THE PLANE TRUTH
Shift Happens at 35,000 Feet

A. Frank Steward

IMPACT PUBLICATIONS
Manassas Park, VA

The Plane Truth

ISBN: 1-57023-211-3

Library of Congress: 2003110550

Publisher: For information on Impact Publications, including current and forthcoming publications, authors, press kits, online bookstore, and submission requirements, visit our website:
www.impactpublications.com

Publicity/Rights: For information on publicity, author interviews, and subsidary rights, contact the Media Relations Department: Tel. 703-361-7300, Fax 703-335-9486, or email: info@impactpublications.com.

Sales/Distribution: All bookstore sales are handled through Impact's trade distributor: National Book Network, 15200 NBN Way, Blue Ridge Summit, PA 17214, Tel. 1-800-462-6420. All other sales and distribution inquiries should be directed to the publisher: Sales Department, IMPACT PUBLICATIONS, 9104 Manassas Drive, Suite N, Manassas Park, VA 20111-5211, Tel. 703-361-7300, Fax 703-335-9486, or email: info@impactpublications.com.

CONTENTS

Dedication

This book is dedicated to the memory of the fallen flight crewmembers of September 11, 2001, and the unspoken heroes on the days that followed. This is also dedicated to all of the airline employees who are currently on the financial roller coaster of uncertainty. Maybe this book can give you a smile or a chuckle as you face the stressful and ever-changing world of air travel. Good luck and never give up hope, for this is all merely part of the journey.

Be Frank!

Acknowledgments

This book would not have been possible without the guidance and invaluable assistance from my "Plane Folks," Mardie and Bob Younglof. I'd like to thank my wife Martha for her love, encouragement, and patience while I chased this dream. A deep appreciation goes out to all the people of Impact Publications for taking a second bet on better timing. Thanks also to Mark Brewster for the illustrations, Irish Stew for the poem, Harry Steward for spreading the Frank word, and the entire Steward family for the kind words out on the line.

Most of all, I would like to thank the airline employees and passengers — you make my world interesting, and, with this book, I hope I have returned a portion of the favor.

The Truth According to A. Frank Steward

Let's be frank, the whole airline industry, passengers and employees, could use a deviation. A break from the constant complaints,
delays, and fears. Events such as 9/11, the war in Iraq, SARS, and
airline mismanagement have painted a truly gloomy picture. I think
it's high time we start putting the word fun back in air travel.

Before take-off I'd like to say a few things. No, I am not going to
tell you how to fasten your seatbelts or where the nearest exit is. I
merely want to offer an insight about the book you are about to read,
an air-map in case you get lost. I am truly a flight attendant and the
stories you are about to read were written as a hobby more so than
for publication. I wrote them while on layovers as a way of captur-
ing the intrigue and hilarity of an often time controversial career. I
kept these stories in a file called Observations and Life Lessons In-
Flight. I don't hold a degree in psychology or philosophy but I
strongly believe that everyone has something to offer in this life,
whether it is knowledge, a different life perspective, or merely an
obscure lesson of some kind. Who else better to tell you the inside
stories on air travel than A. Frank Steward?

When an editor suggested publishing these stories, I laughed it
off thinking of all the reasons not to. In time, I changed my opinion
and persevered. The results were my first book and the one you have
in your hands now. It was September 2001 when *The Air Traveler's*

Survival Guide was published and I was fairly optimistic about my prospects. Unfortunately, September 11th ended any such jubilation. The cover of the book showed a pilot parachuting out the window; in one chapter I claimed that America's airports were a terrorist activity waiting to happen; and my publisher had recently sent out a press release with the opening statement of "Isn't it time we laughed at air travel?" It clearly was not such a time. While my troubles seemed trivial compared to the shock of this atrocity, many aspects of the airline industry, people, and situations instantly changed, so I carried my notebook everywhere I went and this book is the result.

What is being Frank? Well, besides a play on words that I undoubtedly use too much, it's a way of laughing at life in a critical but humorous manner. I grew up reading Robert Fulghum and listening way too much to George Carlin. From their tutelage I have learned that everything in life has an interesting or funny side, even that annoying passenger in 15b. While I do believe that the unexamined life is worth living, I just don't think it's as much fun.

This is not a book to convey my dislikes or dissatisfaction about my career, but, rather, a way of celebrating the experiences that I have encountered along the way. I love my job, I am not a bitter flight attendant, and have no intention of placing you in a bad mood. My one hope is that I can entertain you or make a difference in your travels, as I promote my creed in life of "He who laughs, lasts."

I don't represent any one specific airline and I by no means speak for all flight attendants, but can tell you that there is a little Frank Steward in each and every one of them. Don't feel the need to read this book in one sitting; instead, read a little bit at a time, ideally during flights, airport delays, or layovers. When you're finished with this book, offer it up to a flight attendant who could undoubtedly use a break.

While I do have a current storyteller's license, most of the stories are based on true incidents, with names and certain situations being changed to protect the innocent, guilty, and overtly grumpy. From time to time, I may repeat or contradict myself, or offer an opinion that you may not totally agree with. All of this is covered under the storyteller's license disclaimer, but if you feel strongly about something in the book, feel free to let me know. I can be reached at my website www.franksteward.com. Praise and criticism alike are always welcome, and all I ask is for you to be frank!

Now, sit back, relax, and let's get this journey underway, but beware, the ability to laugh at yourself is strongly recommended. When your overhead bin opens during this flight, shift happens!

Terminal 1

A Frank Take-Off

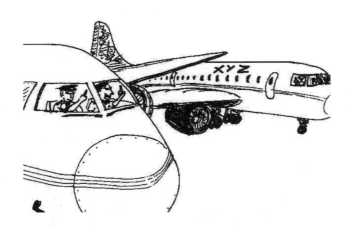

Plane Genuis

Unfortunately, the larger the airline, the less sense of humor the employees are allowed. Major international airlines have to remain politically correct, while the low-cost domestic airlines can get away with humorous announcements, jokes, and even casual uniforms. I work for a major airline and am not supposed to reveal my sense of humor to the passengers. It doesn't necessarily mean I always follow the rules, but that is another matter.

This lack of humor in my airline results in a sterile approach to air travel. Officially, I am not even allowed to say "Merry Christmas" for fear of insulting someone with other beliefs. Such is the case concerning all of the holidays. It may sound ridiculous but it's the truth.

So while the smaller carriers make you laugh, the larger ones try not to offend in any way, shape, or form, and reward you with exotic destinations and frequent flyer points.

Occasionally, though, a few good stories stand out that can't go unmentioned.

The captain for the low-cost carrier, "No Frills," was in a hurry to push back before the plane next to him. It belonged to the major airline, "XYZ," and was scheduled to depart at about the same time. This type of race is a small but harmless game they play up front, so the pilots in the XYZ airplane were most assuredly hurrying as well. The No Frills Captain had previously been furloughed from XYZ, so naturally some spite remained.

When the tower granted No Frills permission to push back first, the captain made the following announcement: "Ladies and gentlemen, welcome aboard. We are happy to have you joining us today. Here at No Frills we like to think of us as the true friendly airline. If you look out your window on the right side, you will see the airline that claims to be of the friendly skies. Please watch the pilots' reaction to us pushing back first."

At that moment, both of the No Frills pilots flipped a blatant middle finger at the two pilots in the XYZ plane. The XYZ pilots returned the gesture with aggressive vigor. What they were unaware of was that more than a hundred passengers were witnessing their actions.

"Now folks, does that look like the friendly skies to you?" Game, set and match!

Victoria's Secret

Most of the flight attendants I fly with today are part-timers. Not to say they don't work a full shift every month, but, rather, they have another job as well. For example, in the course of one month I have flown with crewmembers with secondary jobs such as a stockbroker, nurse, real estate agent, financial planner, and interior designer. The flight attendant profession, with the amount of time off and schedule flexibility, makes it possible to have an additional job. Things get a bit tricky, however, when flight attendants mix work with their secondary jobs. We are not supposed to use our job with the airlines to promote any occupation, solicit customers, or pursue any onboard activity that could lead to personal monetary advancement. We aren't even allowed to accept tips. There are gray areas on the wrongs and rights, but as long as the behavior is discreet and doesn't offend anyone directly, it is usually overlooked.

I've seen flight attendants sell lotion, jewelry, cell phone plans, Amway, and now the latest kick is pre-paid legal services. I even used to fly with two ladies in Pan Am who were high-priced call girls. They called themselves "Ladies of the Flight." They used the airline job for transportation and conducted business on layovers. I'll give you one guess what class of service they preferred to work.

I guess you can say I was using the airlines as a way of getting stories, characters, and material for my books. When my first book was released, I indirectly used flights to get the word out among other crewmembers. Since I was donating a portion of the proceeds to the 9/11 families of flight attendant victims, I didn't see the harm.

On a flight to Europe I decided to test the waters and took the book out of my bag. I walked to the Economy galley where the crew normally gathered. It was after the meal service and most passengers were either asleep or watching the movie.

An elegant looking flight attendant named Victoria was closing the curtains. "Are you in or out?" she asked as I approached.

"In," I responded, confused, not having a clue what was taking place. I tucked the book under my jacket and watched her presentation.

With the curtains shut, six flight attendants gathered around. "Ladies and gentlemen, welcome to Victoria's little secret," she announced in a soft tone, opened her bag, and revealed a small marital aid collection. It consisted of three vibrators, a catalog, and some items that I couldn't quite distinguish.

Some of the flight attendants chuckled, others blushed, and my mouth nearly hit the floor. Victoria was a vibrator saleslady, or, as she preferred to say, a "satisfaction consultant." I was the only one not briefed prior to the presentation, and while some were a bit shy, they gathered closer. "I started doing this when I found out most ladies want, but don't have the courage to purchase, such items. Feel free to take a card and remember that all orders are confidential. Now, I realize this is a personal subject matter, so if you want to talk to me in private, I am available throughout the layover for questions and orders. Does any one have any questions right now?" She looked around.

I pride myself on being able to participate in everything from the girl talk in the cabin to being one of the guys in the cockpit. I consider myself a fairly open-minded person. "I do. What is that?" I pointed to an item with a remote control device.

"Ah, this is what I call a jumbo jet flyer. But seeing that you are married, I don't recommend this for your wife, as this item will replace you. This is more for the woman who is happy being alone, if you know what I mean. If you want a good wife gift, stick with the narrow body." She smiled and went on to the next question.

She had a great sales pitch and a fairly mature approach to such a personal subject. She even had a sign in her bag that indicated 20% of all proceeds were donated to the same charity as mine. On the sign was the slogan, "Feel good and give at the same time." This and "Satisfaction Guaranteed" had all of us in the galley laughing.

"Hey, Frank, what do you have there?" a flight attendant asked, pointing at my book.

"Oh, nothing, just some book that I am reading." I went off to answer a call bell and quickly put away my book. I couldn't, and didn't wish to, compete with Victoria's products. I returned to the galley as the presentation continued. "Hand me some peanuts, Frank." Victoria pointed to the basket of snacks next to me.

I went to grab a pack when all of a sudden something inside the basket started to move and scared the daylights out of me. As I jumped to the other side of the galley, everyone else roared with laughter. I then noticed the remote control in Victoria's hand.

"My biggest seller," she chuckled.

I reiterate that she had a fairly mature approach. She later told me she made twice as much on her sales than she did as a flight attendant. She was a true entrepreneur. Good for her, when opportunity knocks...or should I say, vibrate? A few months later, I heard she got in trouble while going through security. Apparently, two of her items were going off simultaneously. An alarm went off as authorities took apart her bag piece by piece. An in-flight supervisor was called and, needless to say, she now only carries the catalog with her for presentations.

If you're going to pack any mechanical devices, naughty or nice, take out the batteries and put them in your checked baggage to avoid delay and/or embarrassment. Try to limit yourself to one or two items. It's a gadget-oriented world these days, but the more items you bring while flying, the more hassles seem to follow during security checks.

For more information about Victoria and her products, go to my website and click on links — remember, satisfaction is guaranteed.

Inflight Reservation

Jean was a sweet older flight attendant. Her doctor had discovered the prior year that she had had diabetes for most of her life, a condition that she had not been aware of. Once treated, she lost the weight that had always plagued her. She had a fun-loving personality and many wonderful stories to tell. The engagement ring her late husband had given her was now a problem, as her fingers had become slim, and the generously sized diamond constantly made its way toward her palm. She chose to live with the problem instead of fixing it or leaving the ring at home.

On a flight to London, during the breakfast service Jean rolled the cart down the aisle, quietly offering coffee and drinks to the few passengers who were awake. At one point, she swung her arm over a seat and reached for something on the drinks cart. Her diamond hooked onto a passenger's toupee and plucked it off. In horror she thought she saw a rat-like creature crawling up her hand. She started to scream and wave her hand frantically, but the creature did not jump off. All of the passengers awoke and watched in fear as Jean screamed down the aisle, waving her hand ferociously. The other flight attendants and I were in shock as we watched the drama.

She made it to the back of Economy and started to hit the wall in an attempt to kill or seriously injure the attacking creature. She eventually stepped on the hairpiece, pulled her hand free, and disappeared into the nearest lavatory. The cabin became silent, as all eyes were on the extremely embarrassed scalpee. He looked like a convertible caught in a rainstorm. Although many tried to hold back their laughter, few were able to. The man promptly reached into his carry-on bag and pulled out a baseball cap and waved to the crowd good-naturedly.

Jean emerged from the restroom 30 minutes later, gave an apologetic hug to her victim, and received a round of applause from the cabin. She spoke to him for a while attempting to explain, and surreptitiously handed him a sick bag containing the hairpiece. Before landing, Jean presented the man with a bottle of First Class champagne for being a good sport.

The man left the sick bag with hairpiece behind, realizing he could never look at it in the same way again. Fearing the cabin cleaner's reaction when found, Jean kept it as a souvenir of her most embarrassing episode. She eventually got her ring resized, but never lived down her new nickname of "Little Running Hair."

Saying a Mouthful

We had been given the word the airline's CEO was going to be on our flight that day and we were to be on best behavior. I was brand new and scared to death of anyone in upper management. The one saving grace was that I was working in Economy and would probably not see him at all.

Maggie, an older female co-worker, sighed, "I wish I was working up front. I would give him such a piece of my mind. And if he wouldn't talk to me, I'd spit right in his food. He is one of the main reasons that this airline is going under."

Maggie was a fun flight attendant to work with. Her favorite saying was, "I am big, black, and jolly, now leave me alone."

Before boarding, the purser made a PA announcement stating that the CEO was known to come back and talk to the crew during the flight from time to time. If he did, we were reminded to be careful about what we said.

"Good, I hope he does. I got lots to talk to him about," Maggie said with vigor.

I looked at her and smiled but I was now afraid of her too. I was on probation, and during the first six months you can be fired at the drop of a hat. You don't have to be given a reason; you get no appeals or Union representation, just a "Good bye."

The flight went along uneventfully and the service ended, the movie played on, and no visit from "Mr. Big." I had heard that he had a couple of rum and cokes and passed out. I was starving but didn't want to go up to First Class to get a meal in case I ran into our guest. So I searched the galley for an extra meal and found a chicken entrée but no clean silverware. I closed the curtain to the galley and looked around to see my co-worker reading her book. I turned to the wall, grabbed the breast of chicken with my fingers and took a huge bite. It was a bit too big but I persevered regardless.

Seconds later a hand tapped me on the shoulder. I spun around and with great horror I was face to face with the CEO. Instead of fainting, I took a step back, gasped, and began to choke on the half chicken vibrating in my throat. I coughed and gurgled, sputtered and convulsed as Maggie and the VIP looked on. I was able to clear my airway and mouth with one large exhale. It was as if in slow motion my oversized morsel flew across the galley and landed on the CEO's shoes.

I froze in fear, he froze in shock, and Maggie stared with a wide-eyed grin. He looked to Maggie for a reaction.

"He's said just about all that I have to say to you!" she replied.

The CEO kicked the carcass off his shoes and replied an awkward, "Okay, I think I'm done here." He turned and walked away.

Maggie turned to me with joy, gave me a huge bear hug, and rejoiced, " I couldn't have said that better if I had tried. Thank you!"

I hid in the toilet for the rest of the flight and tried to keep the lowest of profiles for the duration of my probation. To this day, 15 years later, I am not very comfortable talking to top management. I guess you could say I get all...choked up!

What Are the Chances?

Imagine if you will, hundreds of different people crammed together in a cylindrical metal tube, off to destinations of adventure, business, or personal matters. They cross a time zone or two, but first they must all pass the twilight zone. Through the years, I have come across some strange and interesting episodes, requests, and facts, which bring me to ask an important question: What exactly are the odds of the following events happening?

> A man and his wife, two daughters, the husband of one of the daughters, and the grandmother, all flight attendants, worked a flight to Asia together. Their son was a pilot working as a first officer on that flight as well. Talk about a family affair.
>
> Not knowing one another, a flight attendant based in New York and another based in Seattle worked a two-

hour flight together in Economy. After the service they sat down and talked about everything from the airlines to families. Through their conversation, they discovered that they were actually mother and daughter. The mother, feeling she was too young to start a family, had given up her baby for adoption at birth. Both had no idea where the other one was, but each recently had expressed interest in locating the other.

We have all experienced the traditional sleeping nods of the head while dozing off sitting in an upright position. One man nodded so hard in-flight that he actually broke a vertebra his neck.

Not telling her husband that she was joining him on his European layover, the pilot's wife took her seat at 1A in First Class as a romantic surprise. What she didn't know was that sitting next to her at 1B was his mistress. After take-off, he found out, and you should have seen his expression. I heard the wife and the mistress became good friends. I also hear the pilot is paying a lot in alimony.

Upon hearing that I was a big fan of movies, a man in First Class asked me what was the worst movie I had ever seen. It was an easy question so I answered quickly. Confused by his cold response, I later discovered the passenger was actually the director of that movie.

I once flew with a 767 all male crew of nine flight attendants. Remarkably, all were heterosexual and married. What made this so odd was that both of the male pilots were gay. If you know the airline business you know that this is truly a one in a million chance.

Did you know that most of the onboard regular coffee is 85% decaffeinated? Which is odd because decaffeinated coffee is only 95% caffeine free. Now when you ask if it is regular or decaffeinated, and I respond with a "yes," you'll know why. The mystery of not getting that coffee buzz onboard is suddenly solved.

A burnt out purser concluded the flight's farewell announcement with "Have a nice day." Not realizing that he still had his finger on the broadcast button, he tried to impress his seat partner with "I am sorry that you are all too stupid to see what a screwed up airline we are." Everyone listened in horror, including the CEO's wife and children. Needless to say, the purser is no longer with that airline.

There was once a pilot who didn't realize his conversation with the captain was being broadcast on channel nine of the passenger entertainment system. The conversation consisted of the detailed description of the sexual encounter between him and one of the flight attendants of that flight.

A flight attendant trying to avoid going to work that day called in a bomb threat from his cell phone. He got cut off the first time, so he tried again. He was apprehended 45 minutes later. Criminally stupid is no way to go through life.

A young Dutch man went to the lavatory in-flight, and instead of the lavatory door, he tried to open the plane's exit door. Even though it is practically impossible to get it open in-flight, the handle rotated to the open position. How many bathrooms have you seen with a big metal handle and a window with the sky in the background?

Quite a few years back, before my time, a man shot his gun into the air signaling the end of duck season. The shot pierced a commercial airplane flying overhead, and some shrapnel hit a passenger in the bottom. The investigation revealed that the victim was, unbelievably, the brother of the man who fired the gun.

Here's another statistic for you: 75% of all in-flight fights are a result of an Economy seat reclining issue. That personal space, albeit small, always seems to be a reason to pick a quarrel.

Ninety-nine percent of flight attendants who are handed a hundred-dollar bill for a four-dollar drink despise you and your attempt to get a free drink. Eight out of ten will actually try to collect the change, just to spite you. I now carry 97 one-dollar bills as a way of countering such attempts. Come on folks, we're not stupid...Okay, most of us aren't.

Most, if not all, flight attendants frown at passengers with oversized carry-on luggage. Fifty percent of the biggest offenders are flight crews on their off time.

"What can I get you to drink?" I asked.
"A coke please," the businessman responded.
We no longer served coke and I was tired of the question, "Is Pepsi all right?" So I merely handed him a Pepsi.
"I'm sorry, I asked for a Coke."
"Same thing," I replied, trying to be cute. I couldn't quite understand why this man went into a fit, until I found out that he was a vice-president of Coca Cola.

"Chicken or Beef," I offered the middle-aged American woman on the aisle.

"Chicken." I handed her the meal and she replied, "Does this have meat in it?"

I was a bit stunned. "Uh, yeah...it's chicken."

I was serving drinks from the bar cart, when a passenger asked for a mixed drink of tomato juice and Scotch. Even for me, an experienced drinker and bartender, this was a bit hard to stomach.

A man actually sued his airline for a bad-tasting in-flight meal. He claimed that the emotional trauma he suffered due to his dining experience lost him a very important client. The airline settled out of court for an undisclosed amount. Now that the airlines rarely feed their passengers, I guess he won't have that problem again.

A flight attendant on his last flight decided he wasn't going to take the normal passenger abuse. He was leaving the airline because he had gotten a once-in-a-lifetime career opportunity. The frequent flyer whom he decided to make an example of ended up as his future employer, or, I guess I should say, ex-future employer.

Two male pilots lost their jobs for flying naked. The flight attendant discovered them after they requested extra paper towels. I wouldn't dare guess on what they were doing or thinking, but it does bring a different meaning to the word cockpit.

Sir Lancelot

I had disposed of my military instilled homophobia after the first year as a flight attendant. My firm belief was, and still is, that there are many different roads to travel in life and no one has the right to pass judgment on another.

Lance was an effeminate flight attendant whom I met a while back on a layover. He had a great sense of humor and a sense of inner peace that I secretly envied. The friendship between a feminine homosexual and a straight man was usually somewhat strained but this wasn't the case for us. While we didn't share the same orientation in some areas of life, we bonded in others. I felt that he had many things to teach me, and whenever I got the opportunity to fly with him, I took it.

Such was the case when I flew with him to San Diego a few years back. He made the flight to the West Coast enjoyable and extremely humorous. My wife, being based in

San Diego, met me on the layover, as did his boyfriend. We "double-dated" as he liked to call it. It wasn't awkward, just good food and great conversation. My wife really liked Lance, but I believe his boyfriend, albeit pleasant, was not too keen on our friendship. But as Lance said, "he'll get over it."

The next day we boarded the return flight home and were greeted by an older captain and a muscular military-type first officer co-pilot, preparing to give the pre-flight briefing. The captain was nice enough, but the other pilot silently stood with his arms folded and a scowl firmly affixed on his face. Our airline was going through extremely difficult financial times and was asking all employees for salary concessions. The pilots' union had agreed but the flight attendants' union did not intend to, claiming inequity of salary averages. So, needless to say, the pilots weren't too keen on the flight attendants at the time and vice versa. After the briefing, Jim, the muscle-bound first officer, spoke for the first time. "You flight attendants better get your shit together and agree to some concessions, or this airline is going down the tubes."

"Uh, Mr. Jungle Jim better mind his own business and not talk about matters that he knows nothing about," Lance said in his most feminine voice.

Jim looked at me for a response, and in shock all I could come up with was "Yeah!"

"That's what I mean. If you don't get it together there won't be any business to mind," Jim had raised his voice to a low holler.

"Look, when the average pilot salary is $240,000 at industry top, and the flight attendant average salary is $36,000, which is well below industry average, it sounds like you have a lot more to lose. Now this conversation is over." Lance turned and walked down the aisle.

Jim looked at me again and I came out with my well-rehearsed "Yeah!" Spoken like a true writer, eh?

The pilot got his bag and turned to the cockpit, mumbling "Faggots."

"Ooh, he included you, Frank. You get to be an honorary fag for the flight," Lance retorted laughingly.

Since the 9/11 tragedy there has been less interaction between pilots and flight attendants. The security procedures involving the closed door have made it difficult, if not impossible, to hang out in the cockpit and chat. Usually it's a shame, but in this case it was a true blessing.

After landing, the captain made a quick exit to catch a connecting flight home. The first officer remained behind to say the passenger farewells. Lance, Sarah, the other flight attendant, and I got our bags together and we walked off after the last passenger.

"So, Lance, do you consider yourself a man or a woman?" Jim quipped while walking behind us on the jet way.

"What do you consider yourself, a gorilla or a human being?" Lance quickly replied.

"Okay, guys, lets just break it up," I said, proud that I didn't merely say "Yeah!" We walked out of the jet way and into the terminal.

"No, I'm just curious if you have always been a fairy?"

Lance turned around and said in a soft tone so as not to startle the people in the terminal, "Have you ever gotten your ass kicked by a fairy flight attendant before?" Jim shook his head as Lance continued, "Well, if you don't shut up, you're just about to." He turned and walked away.

"Give me a break! You?" Jim smacked the side of Lance's head lightly.

Instantly, Lance spun around grabbed his hand and applied some kind of hold that had the macho first officer wincing in pain and brought him to his knees.

"Now, I will take the fact that you are on your knees as an apology, but unfortunately I don't accept favors from pilots." He released the hand and Jim fell backwards. The passengers, Sarah, and I looked on in shock. "Oh, don't be so surprised. Gay people can take martial arts too, you know. I just like to think of my black belt as a dark pink." He turned and we walked away.

The now enraged pilot regrouped and charged towards Lance.

"Oh, here we go!" Lance spun around, dodged a fist, and delivered an elbow to the face and a swift kick to the groin area. "Doing that goes against all my beliefs," Lance said as the pilot fell back again and blood began to stream out of his nose.

Security arrived moments later and the two were escorted away. As per Lance's request, I took names and addresses of some eyewitnesses at the scene. I was interviewed, wrote many reports, and was called to testify at a disciplinary hearing. I did all that I could, but Lance was fired regardless. The kicker to all of this is that even though the pilot started it, he was only suspended.

Lance took it all in stride and remarkably was at peace with the outcome. He started a lawsuit against the airline for false dismissal and after two years settled out of court for job reinstatement, back pay, and an undisclosed monetary amount.

After his first month back to work, Lance called me up to tell me that he had quit. He had planned to leave and go back to school at the time of the incident anyway, but Jungle Jim had provided him with the perfect opportunity and, eventually, the tuition money. Before being a flight attendant Lance had been studying pre-law, and during his lawsuit he had passed the bar and become a full-fledged lawyer.

"Lance, I don't know what to say. You're like...like..."

"I know, I know, kind of like SuperFag, right?" Lance interjected.

"Yeah!" There's that oratorical eloquence kicking in again.

Hot Stuff

Our airplane went mechanical in Mexico City on the way to Costa Rica. The local mechanics declared they didn't have the parts on hand and it would be at least 38 hours before our airplane was going anywhere. The airline decided to hedge its bets and set us free for a 30-hour layover at the Mexico City airport hotel. Now, when one says an airport hotel, they usually mean close by or in the general vicinity of the airport. Not this hotel. This one was about 10 yards past immigration and actually inside the airport. We weren't going to get much sightseeing done on that layover.

Luckily, our Spanish-speaking flight attendant, Jose, was a commuter from a small town outside Mexico City. He asked us if we wanted to go to his house and see the real Mexico. Four of us from the crew, three females and I, accepted with no hesitation. We piled into his VW van and headed for his casa. New places and destinations are so

23

much more enjoyable when accompanied by a local, and this time was no exception. We drove through the city as Jose pointed out landmarks, monuments, and the history of Mexico City. If you can look beyond the poverty and pollution, you will find a city full of quite genuine and kind people.

We arrived at his home and were quite shocked to see his substantial house with an incredible view. In reaction to our amazement, Jose said that while we complained about our meager paychecks each month, his was considered quite healthy in Mexico. We had a beer on his veranda while Jose called for a cab to take us to dinner. Alcohol consumption was a certainty and the penalty for drinking and driving is quite severe there.

We pulled up to a rather large cantina in a small but quite picturesque village, walked inside, and were greeted by mariachi music. Several rounds of "hola Jose" roared from the full bar and half-full dining room. It was like a Mexican version of Cheers welcoming Norm.

Cervezas and margaritas were plentiful, and everyone sang along to the mariachi rendition of "La Cucaracha." The table had chips, salsa, peppers, and a small wooden bowl of what looked like black beads. I picked one up and rolled it around in my fingers, squeezed it until it popped, but it had no smell. I didn't think any more about it.

The dinner started to arrive so I thought I would get washed up for the meal. Now, when a man says he'll get washed up for dinner, it usually means he has to go to the toilet and then wash. There I was, standing at the urinal doing my business while humming a mariachi tune. I started to get a small tingling sensation from down below, followed by a burning and then a sharp painful scorching. I looked down in horror at my hands and remembered the black bead. There is no delicate way to say this, but my crotch area and more specifically its most important resident were on fire. I hobbled over to the sink, stood on my tiptoes, and ran cold water over my groin in panic.

Jose entered the bathroom. "Frank, what the hell are you doing?" he exclaimed in shock.

"The beads, the table, hot, hands, pee..." was all I could muster between splashes.

Jose ran out of the bathroom and re-entered seconds later with a glass of milk. "I know you're going to think I am crazy, but put your thing in this glass. It will help." He chuckled and handed me the glass.

As stupid as it sounded and as silly as I felt, it really helped. The burning sensation subsided and tenderness set in. Jose left to give me a little privacy. After a couple moments of regrouping, I cleaned up my mess and tried to reappear inconspicuously. I opened the door, and everyone, including the locals, shouted "OLE!" The mariachi band played the theme from Rocky (Eye of the Tiger) in my honor, and everyone had a good laugh.

Even though I swore the crew to secrecy, my nickname around the base became "Hot Stuff." Which is a lot better than the alternative of "Jalapenis?"

So the lesson of the story is: First of all, always accept a local's tour offer, and second, when in a foreign country, don't touch what you don't know. It might get you in the end — or in my case, the front. Milk does do a body good, the whole body.

Come to think of it, I could have made a great commercial for the dairy farmers: my wincing face and big bold letters...GOT MILK?

Passenger Address Announcements

Have you ever boarded a flight only to discover that it is under the command of Captain "Boring," or Chief Purser "Comedian"? If you're not sure, here's what they would have sounded like over the P.A.:

Captain Boring: "Ladies and Gentlemen, uuuuuuuhhhhhh, we are currently flying at uuuuuuuuuuuuhhhhhhhhhhhh 35,000 feet, and uuuuuuuhhhhhhhh."
You get the picture.

Chief Purser Comedy Guy: "Hey there, guys and gals, welcome onboard your flight to the beautiful city of angels. Angels? I've may have seen a few fairies there, but can't say I have seen any angels. Thank you, thank you very much, I'll be here all day."
He may think he's funny, but actually he makes you squirm in your seat every time he speaks.

It's not really fair to the flying public because they are a captive audience with no choice but to listen. The no-frills carriers encourage humorous announcements, while the major airlines, fearing repercussions from the Political Correctness Mafia, discourage them. This type of humor hits different people in different ways. If you haven't just been canceled, treated poorly, or held hostage on the runway, humorous announcements can be a source of great stress relief.

The following are examples of some of the better announcements:

BOARDING

Pilot's welcome: "At our airline we are pleased to have some of the very best flight attendants in the industry. Unfortunately, none of them are on this flight today."

Male flight attendant: "Ladies and gentlemen, we aren't anticipating a full flight, so at this time please look around, and if you don't like the looks of the person sitting next to you, feel free to move to another seat in the cabin. Or if you see someone you would rather sit next to — for example, the blonde in row 34 — this is the time to do so."

Pilot: "Sorry about the delay in pushing back from the gate, but apparently they don't take American Express at the gas pumps." The thing that makes this so tragic is it was made in the Pan Am days, and he was not joking. He was in fact using his personal credit card, as Pan Am's credit was gone.

Pilot: "This is such a senior flight that our flight attendants are offering grandmotherly service across the Pacific today."

SAFETY LECTURE

"There may be 50 ways to leave your lover, but there are only six ways to leave this airplane."

"To fasten your seatbelt, insert the metal tip into the buckle and pull tight. If you don't know how to operate one, you probably shouldn't be out in public unsupervised."

"In case of a water-landing, your seat bottom cushion can be used as a flotation device, but, considering the airline never washes them, they will probably smell worse than death anyway. Please paddle to the nearest shore, and keep the cushions with our compliments."

"Should the cabin lose pressure, hopefully oxygen masks will drop from the overhead compartment. Please place the bag over your mouth and nose before assisting children, or other adults acting like children."

"In the event of a sudden loss of cabin pressure, stop screaming, grab the mask and pull it over your face. If you have a small child traveling with you, secure your mask before assisting with theirs. If you are traveling with more than one small child, pick your favorite."

IN-FLIGHT

On a very senior flight, a pilot made the following announcement, "We've reached the cruising altitude and will be turning down the cabin lights. This is for your comfort and to enhance the appearance of your flight attendants and meal choice today."

Note: that pilot obviously didn't have a meal scheduled for the flight.

"Mile High Club applications can be found in the aft lavatories of the Economy section."

"Please use the lavatory in your section. The ones in First Class aren't any different, except for a little linen fold that I can never get right anyway..."

"If you need direction during the flight, a flight attendant would be more than happy to tell you where to go."

"The weather at our destination is 85 degrees with some broken clouds, but we'll try to have them fixed before we arrive. Thank you and remember, nobody loves you, or your money, more than we do."

"And for our meal selection onboard today we have the choice of the brown meaty gook or the white stuff with yellowish sauce. It's the best I can do without a menu in front of me."

"The only place to smoke on today's flight is on the wing, please step through, foot first, and follow the arrows. If you can light em, you can smoke em."

"And on the left side we have a great view of the Grand Canyon. For those of you on the right side we have..., hey, where'd that airplane come from?"

"We are privileged to have our former CEO flying with us today in First Class. He is no longer with us because we have little money left after paying his salary. Won't you join me in wishing him a luxurious and guilt-free retirement?"

"It is time to begin our preparation for landing. Yes, believe it or not, the pilots have actually found the airport this time..."

This classic flight attendant story must be repeated one more time: A snooty passenger in First Class after being treated rudely replied, "Excuse me, do you know who I am?" The flight attendant promptly got on the microphone and announced, "Ladies and gentlemen, we have a person in First Class who doesn't know who he is. If you can help us with this or can claim him, we would be very grateful."

"You complained about the meals so much, we have decided to start charging you for them. The free beef entrée doesn't sound so bad now, does it?"

AFTER ROUGH LANDING

"Please take care when opening the overhead bins because after a landing like that, sure as hell everything has shifted."

Pilot: "I am sorry about that, folks. It wasn't the airline's fault, it wasn't the pilot's fault, it was the asphalt."

As the plane landed, a voice came over the speakers: "Whoa, big fella, whoa!"

"Please remain in your seats while the captain taxis what's left of our airplane to the gate."

"We ask you to please remain seated as Captain Kangaroo bounces us to the gate."

"After all three of those landings, we would like to welcome you to…"

"We have just landed — no, contrary to popular belief, we weren't shot down…"

FAREWELL

"Thank you for flying with us today. We hope you enjoyed giving us the business as much as we enjoyed taking you for a ride."

"As you exit the plane, make sure to gather all of your belongings. Anything left behind will be distributed evenly among the flight attendants. Please do not leave spouses or children, thank you."

"The next time you get the inclination to blast through the skies in a pressurized metal tube, carrying approximately 50,000 pounds of flammable liquid, we hope you will think of us again."

"We hope you enjoyed your flight with us at Pan Am today. If not, thank you for flying TWA."

And finally the one that inspired the subtitle to this book, and my favorite:

"Please be careful retrieving articles from the overhead compartments, as items may have shifted during the flight, because we all know very well that in the airline industry **SHIFT HAPPENS!**"

Airport Walks of Life

Walking through the airport on any given day can seem like an arduous or mundane task but have you ever noticed the many different varieties of airport walks there are out there?

First, there is the ever-popular **I-am-Late-for-My-Flight Gallop**. This is the one where all humility and grace are lost. It is the sweat pouring, hair's a mess, bumping into anyone in their path scramble. It used to be called "pulling an O.J. Simpson," but that is now reserved for quite a few other things. The only thing worse than being trampled by this person is sitting next to them on the airplane as the sweat undoubtedly reminds you of the need for travel anti-perspirant.

The Cell Phone Shuffle – No urgent destination, just shuffling along and talking. Meanwhile, a trail of late-flighters are behind them, trying to get by, fantasizing where they'd like to put that phone. One more thing to note on this point, do cell phone users think that the other people around them can't hear their side of the conversation? Think about this the next time you're talking about the details of a recent enema.

The Gate Dysfunctional Stammer – This is the person who seems to stop and stare at every gate and flight information monitor in the airport making sure they don't pass their flight. Most of the time they start looking around Gate 10 while their flight is a mile down the concourse in the 70's. It is especially frustrating if you are forced to walk behind them for any length of time.

The Non-Moving Walker – How about those moving walkways? What is it about the name that confuses people so much? Moving, as in motion, and walkway, as in a way to walk. You just got off or are about to get on an airplane where you will be sitting down. This is not a ride at some amusement park; don't just stand there, GO! I actually don't have a problem with those of you who wish to stand, but don't look at me as I pass as if I am a pest who is breaking the rules. On the same subject, doesn't it seem odd that most moving walkways are either broken or not moving? Why does everyone purposely avoid the moving walkways when they are not moving? It doesn't mean you can't still walk on them as a way of a less congested trail. The next time you walk on a broken walkway, notice that, when you get on or off, your body still fools you into believing that it was moving.

The I-Hate-My-Travel-Agent Cadence – This is a slow but decisive directional walk with attitude which is due to the travel agent having booked an extremely long airport wait between flights. Either that or they missed their tightly scheduled connections and have to wait for the next flight five hours later.

The Blue Polyester Story Group Migration – This is where a flight attendant is telling a story on the way to a flight and everyone else in the group wants to hear. Add their suitcases with wheels and you have quite a tough obstacle to get around. I have seen giraffe migrations move faster.

The Center-of-the-Universe March – This is where the person heading towards you refuses to alter his direction and expects the other people to move. I always try to maintain my heading but flinch out of the way at the last second. Then there is the complete opposite to the previous one, the dance. This is where the person heading towards you moves to avoid you and you move in the same direction to avoid them. When it happens more than two corrections, you're dancing.

The Maternal Movement – This is the mother who has three small kids and four huge bags. She manages to deafen all who pass with her high-pitched screams to her kids, which undoubtedly makes people reconsider their plans for procreation.

The Groper – This is the man who fails to realize his new well-fitted suit does not compensate for his lower region readjustment problem.

The Obsessive-Compulsive Stumble – This is performed by the person who puts everything into several bags with many compartments. They stop every third step to recheck their passports, tickets, and personal belongings on the way to the gate. While this ritual is annoying, I have to admit that I am guilty of this from time to time.

The Baywatch Bounce – When you are late for a flight you are late for a flight and undoubtedly forget about certain restrictions you may have in life. Some women with big chests aren't used to running in the attire that they may be wearing. When the concourse is full and she comes running down the terminal, you can bet that many eyes are bouncing with her. I must be getting older as it doesn't intrigue me as much as it makes me wince at the pain that sometimes must be involved

Alas, the walk that angers me the most is that of the Stoppers. These are the people who at any given moment stop suddenly, dead in their tracks. Whether it be for duty-free shopping, ticket questions, gate info, or whatever, everyone has a duty to slowly step to the side and then stop, rather than causing a potentially dangerous chain reaction. The amount of times that I have had to stop short and the person behind me unloads their Grande Latte on my back, is staggering. We can't forget the British and their insistence to walk on the wrong side of the traffic flow, unless of course you're in England.

Last but not least, we have the **Seat Picker**. No, not the one who chooses where to sit. This is the one who has undoubtedly been flying for many hours and deems it necessary to walk and readjust the underclothes that have obviously been swallowed up by their bottom. What is the old saying? "You can pick your friends but don't pick your seat," or was that "nose"? Whatever it is, don't do it in front of me or the hundred passengers behind you. Head for the bathroom. All of us thank you.

Walk On!

Seize the Day

My wife, Martha, hung up the phone and grinned at me suspiciously. It was one of those grins that usually came along with a far-fetched idea like let's move or change our life in some way. She told me the pilot who was renting the plane to take a certain dream trip canceled at the last minute, and she wanted us to go instead. She didn't tell me where or what it was, just that it was a surprise and to pack my overnight bag.

My wife is an excellent pilot and I have all the faith in the world in her abilities, but until then I was always the silent nervous passenger on the two-hour flights we took. The words "overnight" and "something new" were what troubled me, but I threw caution into the wind and complied.

We took off in a twin Comanche four-seater airplane and headed east with a packed lunch and Nikon camera at our side. I was normally the traffic spotter when I wasn't sightseeing. The weather was beautifully clear and there were no signs of the humidity or haze that typically hung around in August.

We passed over Atlantic City, but as I expressed my excitement of having never been there, Martha just smiled and shook her head as we continued north. An hour later, I spotted a big bridge and two helicopters.

"Okay, Frank, this is it. Get the camera ready," Martha said.

It was the Verrazano Bridge and beyond that was New York's impressive skyline. We flew 500 feet above the Statue of Liberty and continued up the Hudson River. I had flown into New York hundreds of times, but never had I seen it like this. I feverishly clicked away as we approached the skyscrapers.

"How is this legal?" I mused.

"As long as we remain below a thousand feet and report our location, we're fine."

We flew above our layover hotel and directly beside the World Trade Center. The two towers loomed over us as I took pictures and waved childishly to the people inside. The morbid side of me thought this had to be a terrorist activity waiting to happen, a thought I now wish I had not had.

A C130, military equivalent to a 747, flew overhead and provided us with a little clear wake turbulence. I broke my trance but was completely stunned at what we had just done. An hour later we arrived at Block Island and enjoyed a romantic night of lobster, wine, and lovely accommodations.

One month later, the 9/11 tragedy occurred and civilian aircraft will never repeat that plane trip. Ironically, on September 13th we got back our pictures of our wonderful adventure. The memories they were supposed to provide were now overshadowed by grief and the terrible loss of life.

The pilot, who had always dreamed of taking the trip, canceling for whatever reason, will now never be able to. Thousands of people went to work on September 11 and, through no fault of their own, would never accomplish certain dreams they had aspired to.

Whatever reasons you have for delaying certain adventures or dreams, don't procrastinate--fulfill one or two of them now!

You never know when the chance may be gone forever.

Terminal 2

Reaching Crewsing Altitude

Uniformity

A famous comedian once said, "If you are at work and wearing a name tag, then somewhere along the line, you probably made a serious error in career choices." When I heard this, I was at the airport, and not only did I have a name tag on, I was wearing a tie that matched the curtains on the aircraft. I started to look back on my life and couldn't actually remember a job where I didn't have a name badge of some kind. Even when I was in a jazz band, our shirts and jackets had our names embroidered on the chest. According to the comedian, my whole life had been a series of career choice errors. I quickly removed the name tag and never wore it again. That'll show him.

Flight attendants are known as the polyester people. While variations in uniforms occur among airlines, many similarities remain, such as luminescent ties and scarves, vests, and serving jackets. I think the airlines want to make sure we don't wear the uniform on our off-time. They can rest assured that we don't. Nobody in the airline industry is ever crazy about their uniform, but some have it better than others. For example, when I am in a three-piece polyester suit in the heat of summer, the humidity makes the fabric feel like it is melting onto my skin. Then, at the pinnacle of my frustration, a flight attendant from a "no-frills" airline walks by in shorts, tennis shoes, and a casual shirt, as cool as can be.

"How unprofessional and low class," I mumble under my breath. Is what you hear the distinct ring of envy? Of course it is. What I wouldn't give to be able to wear casual attire on an airplane. To add insult to injury, I have to put an apron on when I start the service!

With the new trend of low-cost carriers, I feel that many changes to the uniform are coming. I wouldn't be surprised if the flight attendants were eventually required to wear a costume of some kind and perform in the aisles. Didn't I hear something about a Hooters' Airline?

The pilots wear their military-looking uniforms with epaulets, and caps resembling those of sky porters. I assume airline uniform designers haven't quite grasped the idea of women in aviation yet. When I see female pilots in uniform, they usually look awkward and like little boys to me. Granted, some do look like men in real life, but that's a different subject.

On longer flights, the crews get in-flight rest breaks, sometimes lasting up to three hours. Some of the airplanes have a section with bunk beds, located away from the passengers. It can make all the difference on a 14-hour flight. I am not senior enough to get those trips very often, but once in a blue moon I get lucky. The first time I did, I discovered that many crewmembers, accustomed to such trips, wore pajamas. People donned everything from flowing night-gowns to nightwear with feet attached. I settled into my bunk for a long rest. Upon waking, I discovered five flight attendants my grandmother's age taking off their nighties and getting back into their uniforms. No man, straight or gay, should be subjected to that. Oh, I know, grow up! It's just that some images never quite leave you.

Every airline has regulations on how to wear the uniform correctly. You say, what's the big deal? Shoes on the feet, tie around the neck, and so on, right? Many people, in search of an individual identity, want to push the limit. Some female flight attendants hem their dresses too short, so, when they reach up and close the overhead bins, passengers get more than an eyeful. Some wear their hair in a crow's nest and others have comb-overs. One flight attendant wears her scarf around her head as a headband. She looks like she is going to war; who knows, maybe that's how she feels about her job.

Some flight attendants wear items that they're not supposed to, complain about their uniform, or plead for apparel improvements. In my opinion, it's just a uniform. In my lifetime, I have worn uniforms resembling everything from a tree to an animal. It beats having to buy your own clothes, thus keeping up with expensive fashion trends. You may not like what you wear to work, but it could always be worse, except, maybe, for people at the shopping malls with the colorful hot dog hats.

According to the in-flight regulations, we can't have visible tattoos, excessive jewelry, abnormal body piercings, and we must adhere to the uniform guidelines. One airline's uniform code states clearly that all flight attendants must wear proper under-garments at all times, including panties and bras. While this may settle well with some male flight attendants, please don't make me do it. I promise to put the name tag back on!

Politically Incorrect

The congressman was the last to board the flight. I was a passenger in the First Class seat next to him. We had been waiting on him to close the doors and get on our way. The plane took off, and he and I had a couple of cocktails together and engaged in polite conversation. Before the meal service, a man from the Economy section brought his six-year-old son up to meet the political figure.

"Hey, sonny, what do you want to be when you grow up?" the slightly inebriated congressman said as he patted the boy on his head.

"I want to be a pilot or a senator just like you!"

"Well, you'd better stay in school or else you may end up being a flight attendant instead," he said, as I almost choked on an ice cube.

Okay, Mistake #1: Besides being someone who needs to watch what he says, he hadn't eaten yet, and a flight attendant working the flight overheard the comment. I pondered the path his entrée would take before it got to him.

Mistake #2: Never underestimate a stranger sitting next to you. I was nice about it, knowing I had heard worse.

Mistake #3: I don't care what your views are. Simply keep your strong beliefs and comments to yourself.

We continued talking through another cocktail, but now I was defensive and ready for anything. The pilot came out of the cockpit to use the lavatory. She was pretty, black, and fairly young. I looked at the congressman's face and saw the scowl appear.

"You see that pilot?" He continued as he leaned closer, "The only reason she is up there is because of affirmative action."

I could not believe a man who is supposed to be a people person was talking like this. I don't care how much alcohol he had had — there was no excuse for that kind of behavior. He was speaking to a complete stranger. I could have been a reporter, or better yet...a writer.

It all came to a halt when he asked the question I had been waiting for. "So what do you do for a living?"

"Actually, I am a flight attendant," I replied.

He began to stir in his seat as I could tell he was getting uncomfortable.

"And the pilot you mentioned...she's my wife." She wasn't, but I felt it was the perfect knockout punch.

There ended the conversation. It was the first time I had seen a politician at a loss for words. He remained silent for the remainder of the flight.

Commuting Through Life

A person's home is their castle, and wherever they may find that castle, is where they shall call home. Does one risk the quality of their castle to be closer to work? Or do they sacrifice the hours commuting to and from work each day, in order to afford a more substantial and enjoyable castle? It's a catch-22 that is a reality for approximately 75 percent of all modern day workers.

We all know the typical traffic commuters — the ones with the self-help tapes, cell phones glued to their ears, chain smokers, hurry up-and-waiters — that endure the packed roads each day and night. But the commuters I am most familiar with are the airline employee commuters. These are the ones in uniform, waiting at the gates for their names to be called. Most of the time they look as if a good sleep is in order. They may be based in and work out of New York, but they could live in San Diego or even farther away.

They get up early on the morning of a trip, fight traffic to the airport, fly space available with a possible multi-connection destination, and wait around for hours to work an eight-hour international trip. They end up sleeping the whole layover and do the whole scenario in reverse back home. I guarantee you that most of these people end up hating their jobs. But it is the risk they take. The routine works for some, but not so well for others.

Approximately 250,000 pilots and flight attendants work for commercial airlines, of whom 40 percent are considered commuters. That's an amazing 100,000 people. The usual scenario is a one-leg trip from city to city, but I have seen the more severe cases of international commuting. One female flight attendant is based in New York but lives in Seoul, Korea, and another commutes from Miami to Australia. There is even one who works out of Frankfurt, Germany and lives in Canada. This may not sound as extreme as the others, but let me give you a run-down on her commute. After working several trips in a row, she finishes in Germany and boards a 13-hour flight to San Francisco. She then catches a flight to Vancouver, Canada, waits around a couple of hours for a 19-seater express flight, which she gets on only 50% of the time. She lands and then drives 40 minutes to her home, where she pays the nanny most of her paycheck. Why would anyone put themselves or their family through that? She says it's because she wants the quality of life for her daughter. What kind of quality is it for the child when her mother is always grumpy and away from home most of the time? It's hard to believe it is worth all the stress and exhaustion.

On one flight I ran into an old friend whom I hadn't seen in years. After nine years, she was still commuting from San Diego to London, England. I barely recognized her, for the long-distance commute had aged her tremendously. All the miles, time zones, and stress can't be healthy, not to mention the stain it must put on her work record if she misses a flight.

Things get more difficult for commuters when peak travel season arrives and there is no space available for these stand-by fliers. It sounds like a crazy way to live their lives, but that is not for me to say. If you look at the other side of the coin, the commuters value quality of accommodation and affordability that is possible because of commuting. They avoid spending every last penny on extremely high mortgages for less-than-comfortable houses.

To research this subject more closely, I took a notepad to the gate of a popular commuter flight. I chose that destination because 20% of my base lives and commutes from there. All commuters know each other, and, more importantly, they know each other's seniority. The more senior they are, the higher their chances are of getting on the flight. They will usually be in uniform chatting with one another at the gate. One will spot a senior commuter walking towards them in the concourse, and all will roll their eyes as one more seat is taken from them. They'll smile courteously, but hope that no more follow. It's a game of chance with seniority dates and seats available. If they don't make that flight, they will undoubtedly have a back-up flight, route, or accommodation. Unfortunately for these specific commuters, my airline decided to cut all of the six flights a day from the schedule. Now these commuters are forced to either transfer, move, or find alternative routes.

From a distance, the jet-setting lifestyle may sound exciting, but the hours and wasted moments are a bit more than I can comprehend. This is one case to file under the column of "different strokes for different folks," but I guess it can also go under "home is where the heart is."

The New Plane Smell

It was truly a glorious day for my airline, crew, and passengers, for we were flying on the newly delivered state-of-the-art Boeing 777 aircraft. The first 777 flight had taken place a half year earlier, but today was this specific airplane's first passenger flight. I was the purser and happy to be on a new plane for a change. I was used to working the older 747s and had difficulty ever imagining them as new. The airplane was immaculate, every aspect appearing to have that shine of newness. It even had a "new car" smell.

Our captain on that flight was infamously known as "The Narrator," due to his long and drawn out announcements. This day was no exception and he would undoubtedly have much more than usual to say. He started the announcements with the fuel facts, the flying statistics, and then on to the differences that this model brought to the world of aviation. While we were excited as well, the passengers were unable to watch the movie or sleep. It got so bad that they started to complain.

I went up there to politely pass on the growing fury, but couldn't spoil this man's fun. He had a wide ear-to-ear grin, like a little kid on Christmas morning. I glanced over at the younger first officer. He looked kind of green and was wiping the sweat off his forehead in a slightly embarrassed manner. The captain took no notice of this and kept on jabbering away to me about the airplane.

All of a sudden the first officer made a mumbling remark like, "I don't feel so...." He made a motion to get out of his seat in a hurry but failed to remember that he still had his seatbelt fastened. He feverishly unbuckled the clasp, tried to get up, and proceeded to vomit all over the flight deck console.

We all stood there in shock, staring at the thoroughly doused panel. I quickly excused myself, grabbed a stack of paper towels, and let them deal with the little crisis on their own. I may have to deal with upchucking in the cabin but I don't get paid enough to tidy up cockpits.

It could have been somewhat of a dangerous situation, as the acid in the stomach has the potential to severely damage such circuits. The second officer was made to clean up the mess thoroughly, the "new airplane" smell was gone, and the wind was completely taken out of the Narrator's sails. Needless to say, there were no further announcements made from the cockpit.

Just a quick add on: The repair to the panel came to a whopping bill of $75,000. I have always wondered if the airplane's warranty covered such incidentals.

The Awakening

In my 15 years in the flying industry, I have come across many frightening episodes. Oddly enough, the single most petrifying event of my flying career took place during initial training. I was naïve, young, and surrounded by beautiful women. I did what I was told and tried not to stand out too much in class. The day before, I had a hard time staying awake during an eight-hour mock evacuation, and looked forward to the easy-sounding session the following day. It was scheduled as the makeover/demo day. How hard could it be to point at a few exits and talk about skin lotions?

Out of 100 students, 90 were women, 8 of the 10 men were gay, the only ones left were me and the homophobic stud from Chicago who told a gay joke any chance he could to ward off any false notions. I didn't really fit into any one group, so I remained a smiling wallflower. The only studying required for the next day was not to put on any facial products, which was easy because I didn't have any.

The next day I walked to the specified gymnasium with my two roommates, and while I couldn't put my finger on it, they looked a bit different. As we got closer, we joined the rest of the trainees. The women whom I had spent the last 40 days with looked like they had hangovers, to put it kindly. I barely recognized any of them.

Suddenly, it dawned on me that no facial products meant no make-up. I never realized until that day how much the female species relied on cosmetics. The majority of the women didn't like being forced out in public without their miracle lotions and tonics. Depressed, embarrassed, and resembling the zombie scene in Dawn of the Dead, we made our way to class.

The extremely large auditorium was divided into two parts. Half was filled with a hundred students without make up and practicing the safety demo in unison. I laughed as I thought of an old Far Side cartoon that was playing out in front of me. The other section contained the cosmetology booths that were set up for consultations and evaluations. I had an extremely effeminate male consultant who asked me questions and gave me information that I didn't quite understand.

"What lotions and bases do you use?"

"Uh, I don't," I politely replied.

"When is the last time you had a pedicure, manicure, or facial?"

"Twenty-two years." I was 22.

"Nail products?"

"Oh I usually bite them off."

After a great deal of disgust and mild ridicule, I was

sent away with a box of products worth over $200, which was promptly deducted from my first paycheck of $240. With a little help from my roommates, I learned the basics of skin care and proper hygiene.

I laugh when I think about that episode now, but can honestly say that it was an eye-opening and slightly disturbing day. From that moment onward, I realized how lucky I was to be male, a point my wife reminds me of, day in and day out.

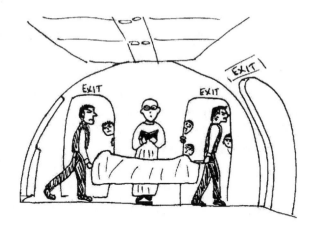

Final Departures

With the schedule flexibility, flying preferences, and off-time, a flight attendant could transfer, retire, or quit, without much notice from fellow co-workers. Death notifications are usually done via the company newsletter. If the flight attendant is not retired at the time of death, a picture is often placed somewhere in the office along with the sad notification. Many times it's hard to recognize the deceased because the picture is usually quite different from the way they looked at work and in uniform.

There was a feisty older lady once who had specifically asked for a certain picture to be displayed if she passed away. In the picture she was sticking out her tongue with her hands on her ears. Everyone laughed hysterically when they saw it. That's the way I would like to be remembered, with a chuckle instead of a tear.

June was a lady whom I remembered by sight and not by name. As I looked at her picture, nothing stood out ex-

55

cept the circumstances of the accident. She was working up in First Class on a hot day. The air conditioner was broken, so, before boarding, an airplane door in front and one in back remained open to provide cross ventilation. On a 747 airplane, the distance between the ground and the door is approximately 32 feet. June was having a debate with Pete, another flight attendant, about the height.

"I'll bet it's 55 feet," Pete remarked.

"Nonsense, 30 tops!" she replied.

"You're way off!"

"Look, all you have to do is gauge…" June walked over to the door and disappeared.

Pete, in shock, ran over to the door and stared down. June was sprawled out on the pavement.

She survived but broke her neck in two places. Five years of rehabilitation later she returned to work. On her third flight, she was working in Business Class and noticed the airline, even after her accident, continued the practice of leaving the doors open. She started to complain vigorously. A junior flight attendant had heard the story and asked her if it was true and, if so, what exactly happened.

"I'll show you. Come with me." June took the junior flight attendant to the front open door, as the morbidly curious followed. "I was walking towards the door like so, and lost my footing and…" when incredibly she lost her footing and fell out the open door once again. She wasn't as lucky this time and died.

Can you imagine the expression on the bystanders' faces? Talk about a real-life re-enactment. From that point on, no doors would be left open without a safety strap. That strap in Pan Am was appropriately named the "June Strap."

I do feel death is tragic, but I also feel that some cases are worth a second glance. The following is a closer look into a few odd but true flight crew departures.

On a Frankfurt layover, two male flight attendants challenged one another to a late night race across the Rhine River. They had had a night of too much German beer and the current was way too strong. They both drowned and were discovered two miles away. The unfortunate outcome makes a strong case that drinking and the term "double-dare" do not mix.

There once was a flight attendant who used to brag there wasn't a hotel window she couldn't open. While on a layover in Japan, she unlocked her window to have a cigarette, leaned out too far, and fell 30 floors to her death, providing yet more proof that smoking is dangerous to your health.

How about the pilot who rented a wood chipper to dispose of his flight attendant wife? The only reason the FBI caught him was that, while trying to save 15% on the rental, he used his Union credit card instead of paying cash. You see, being cheap can be criminal.

What about the flight attendant who discovered that her pilot husband was cheating with countless co-workers? Let's just say the investigation was not highly publicized due to the delicate issues involved, some of which were that the body was never found and the flight attendant was known to bring homemade sandwiches for passengers and crew on flights without meal services. Talk about getting rid of the evidence.

Then there was the case of a flight attendant who prided herself on the amount of water that she drank in-flight. It would not be unusual for her to drink up to six liters of water in one flight. She bragged and lectured on the importance of water consumption. Unfortunately for her co-workers, her work was constantly interrupted by frequent visits to the lavatory. One flight, in an attempt to break her record, she downed an incredible 10 liters of water. Afterwards, she felt unwell and went to the lavatory where she died. I had never heard of over-dosing on water, but the official cause of death was that she had passed out and choked while being sick. The unofficial cause of death was drowning.

A 78-year-old flight attendant always insisted that someday she would die on an Italy layover. One day she showed up for her Rome flight but returned home when the flight was canceled. She passed away the very next day. Sometimes canceled flights ruin our plans as well.

But the most bizarre case that I have ever heard of is the flight to Europe where the plane took off with a crew of four pilots and landed with only three. Somewhere on his break, a pilot wandered off and was never heard from again. The authorities took apart the plane but have yet to solve the case. In an attempt to put the case behind them, the airline authorities determined that he was suffering from depression along with several alimony payments and must have slipped off as a passenger in hopes of a new life. There was no record of him going through customs or immigration, and his bags were all still onboard. Who knows? Maybe he flushed himself down the toilet.

Ahh, respect for the dead. Not a laughing matter you might say? Well, the way I figure it, we are all going sooner or later, so we might as well laugh at death instead of fearing it.

April Foolish

April Fools Day was always one of my favorite days of the year. It wasn't an official holiday but on my calendar it was. Being raised by the likes of Hawkeye and BJ from the sitcom M*A*S*H, I was taught that all was fair in war and practical jokes. The more elaborate the prank, the better. I would begin scheming in January for the events on April 1st. I usually gave better than I got, but have been the butt of many great practical jokes. Nothing could put a damper on my excitement of the glorious day, until one April Fools Day, something went terribly wrong.

Mark was a good friend and fellow flight attendant. He was engaged to Sarah, also a flight attendant, and due to marry on April 10th. His bachelor party was set for March 31st, the night before my special day. After careful research and planning, I devised the ultimate prank. This would be my masterpiece of all other April Fools pranks.

Mark was an avid lottery player. Conveniently, there was a drawing the night of his bachelor party. We went to the party and I took his wallet as a gesture that he was not to pay for anything. That night, after the winning numbers were announced, I snuck out of the party. I purchased the next week's lottery ticket and replaced his old ticket with the new one consisting of the night's winning numbers. This way, when Mark sobered up the following morning, he would check his ticket and believe he was a millionaire. Everything worked without a hitch. I slipped the wallet back into his jacket and got drunk with the rest of the crowd.

The telephone woke me up the following afternoon around 3 p.m. It was Al, Mark's best man, who had helped on the prank. He told me of the incredible events following Mark's rude awakening. Mark had checked his ticket and, after an hour of screaming for joy, continued on a dangerous venting spree. He called up his supervisor at work, told her where she could shove his pathetic job, and what he thought of her and the stupid company. Which, to put it mildly, wasn't good. He then phoned Sarah and postponed the wedding indefinitely until he could "sow his wild playboy oats." Mark then proceeded up the stairs, knocked loudly, and urinated on his landlord's front door. His new millionaire status had just kicked in when he noticed the date on the ticket, and eventually the reality of the prank. Mark was reportedly in a very bad way and not taking it well at all.

"Oh, shit!" was all I could muster as I wracked my hungover brain for a solution.

I called Sarah on her cell phone and she was crying. "You tell that bastard he can go to hell."

When I phoned Mark, a very depressed voice answered, "Hello?"

"I...I don't know what to say. I am so sorry. It was just an April Fools prank."

"You've ruined my life and you think it's funny?"

"No, not at all. I just thought that I...."

"My God, what have I done?" Mark began to cry.

"I promise you I will rectify all of this. I'll undo all that has been done!"

"No, it's too late! I'm outta here," Mark calmly replied and hung up the phone.

I had heard those words before from a friend's suicide note. The situation was getting way out of control. I tried to call him back but the phone was off the hook. I ran into the streets and down the road. Mark lived about three miles away. I ran a mile before I managed to hail down a cab. The traffic was a nightmare and my chest began to grow tight. I folded my head into my hands and pondered the severity of the situation.

"This can't be happening!" I rocked back and forth in my seat.

"Hey buddy, you all right?" the cab driver inquired nervously.

"Yeah, you just have to get me there as soon as humanely possible."

He took a back road and pulled up in front of Mark's apartment moments later. The elevator was out of service, so I scaled the five floors of stairs in seconds. I pounded on the door but heard no answer. I busted through the unlocked door and fell flat on the living room floor. I was greeted by Mark, Sarah, Al, and about five other friends, holding full champagne glasses yelling in unison, "April Fools!"

They laughed and cheered as I tried to regain my composure. I was in shock and couldn't quite grasp the situation at first. There I was, in the best of hangover attire, frayed hair, beads of sweat pouring down my face, and a pounding echo in my head. Al was bragging about his added touch of the "out of order" sign on the lobby elevator.

Apparently, Mark was initially fooled when he checked the ticket but discovered the date soon after. Then he devised the joke to teach me a lesson. Boy, did I ever learn my lesson. I don't think I ever quite got over it. I still have palpitations just thinking about it and, to this day, refrain from celebrating April Fools.

Now the hard part: In the past I have played quite a few practical jokes on April 1st. Some of them were brilliant and well taken, and others have cost me some valuable friends. To those who have suffered, I apologize and hope you can take comfort in the fact that the last joke was on me. Elaborate jokes or pranks can be great fun, but be sure you consider all ramifications and never be too far away from the action so as not to let it get out of control.

Take it from me, the former April Fool.

Boys of Blondin

We were based in London with Pan Am, five male flight attendants living fraternity style in a two-bedroom house on Blondin Ave. We were paid so little that we would have qualified for food stamps in the States, but we were in England. The pound rate vs. the dollar was horrible and of course we were paid in U.S. dollars, which worsened our financial status. So we were forced to improvise.

We bought groceries in the States on layovers, took necessities off the airplanes after flights, and shared extremely cramped living quarters. We were always coming and going on four-day trips, so we rarely were all home at the same time. Although we were short of beds when we were all there, nobody minded because we were the only items necessary for a party. It always amazed me that with the dire financial problems we all had, there was always enough money for beer and pubs.

We were all in our twenties, looking for adventure and good times while we pondered our future and the meaning of life. We shared the same basic hobbies — travel, tennis, drinking, and chasing women. We didn't regard the flight attendant job as a long-term career. It was our form of backpacking across Europe while we figured out what to do with our lives. Pan Am was not expected to last much longer, so we lived for the moment.

The house was decorated with a horrible blue shag carpet, typical bachelor pad posters, and a sparse collection of second-hand furniture. If that sofa could have talked, it would have screamed. You learn a lot about people living in a house with rooms the size of walk-in closets — maybe a bit too much.

Phillip was the wiry ex-drummer who needed to be doing something every minute of the day. His motto was, "Sleep when you're dead." He had the best luck with the women, always bringing someone home to torture us through the thin walls. There was nothing he couldn't build. He never washed his dishes and disregarded our complaints when he smoked in the house. He claimed he blew the smoke out of the window, even though most of the time they were closed.

Dan was the studious type, with non-flattering glasses, always in some corner reading an oversized book. He only ate cereal, morning, noon, and night. In his eyes it was the perfect meal. He was in love with every female who held a hint of Oriental. He didn't like to drink casually. It was drink to get drunk or not at all. When he did get drunk he would break out of his shell, which was a bit too much for us to handle. The next morning it was back to the books and his reserved, inward ways.

Albert was the straight-laced penny-pinching type. He always evaluated the price of everything. The stock market was his favorite section of the newspaper, even though he didn't own any stocks. He complained about most everything British. His humor was so dry that you were never quite sure if he was joking or not, so you laughed at everything he said, just in case. He was a proud member of the grumpy morning coffee club.

Randy was the debater of the group. You would say black and his favorite comeback was, "yes and no," going on to explain why it could be white. He was the big brother to all our female friends, therefore he never had much luck with romance. Randy was the founder of the grumpy morning coffee club. If you spoke to him in the morning, you made sure his coffee cup was full. He was voted the most likely to marry first because of his older-brother personality.

As the youngest of the group, I was the annoying one who was always in a perky morning mood. The comedian even when nobody wanted to laugh. I was always game for anything going. I claimed to be an up and coming writer, so the others gave me the single room, a transformed storage closet, in exchange for promising to mention them in one of my books. My relationships never lasted very long and I was voted most likely to marry last, if at all.

A perfect day for us would be a coffee huddle in the morning, play a tennis tournament during the day, pints at our favorite pub, late night fish and chips, and video games before bed. What more did one need?

This lasted for two years until our base was taken over by a new airline, which offered us jobs. We accepted and agreed among each other to put in transfers to Miami. There the plan of action would be to play tennis, fly to South America, chase women, and drink beer. The same as we were doing in London, just in a warmer climate. We waited six months for the base to open. In the meantime I had met a British girl named Martha, and Albert decided the heat of Florida wasn't for him, so we waved goodbye to the other three.

Years passed, and we kept loosely in touch. We are all still flight attendants but in different corners of the world. Phil married, had a baby, got divorced, and lives happily in Florida. Dan is married to a Thai lady and lives in Bangkok with two daughters. On U.S. layovers I am sure he stocks up on his cereal supply. Albert got tired of complaining about England, married a local, has a baby girl, and is the only one left in Britain. He still whines about the high prices. Randy is the only one yet to marry, even though voted most likely to marry first. He went on to be an avid golfer, claiming it was the only love needed in his life, yes and no. Ironically, I was the first to marry. My excuse for not moving to Miami became my greatest treasure, but Martha and I eventually moved back to the States eight years later.

When I reminisce, I smile and take refuge in the fact that "Those were the good ole days." No responsibilities, no worries, and absent was the stress of things to come. Why is it that the most desperate of times hold our fondest memories? We only remember the good times and let the bad fade away. We constantly bickered about dishes, smoking, money, and living conditions, yet they were great times. Maybe the beauty of memories is that they are selective and, truthfully speaking, I wouldn't have it any other way. I now sit back at my computer in a house five times bigger than the place on Blondin Avenue and considerably less occupied, and realize that it is not what you have in this life, but whom you have to share it with that counts. Luckily, I am very fortunate in that respect as well.

To the boys of Blondin, this one is for you and thanks for the room. I miss you and look fondly on the memories of the "good ole days."

Tennis, anyone?

The Lady in Fred

He was Michael by day and Michelle by night. Our airline hired him as a male and would not recognize his preference to be female until the specific surgery was completed. Apparently, he was unsure of his commitment to go through with the surgery, so he took some time to think matters over. Even if it did interfere with the big picture, I can also imagine that he may have been a little more than sentimentally attached to the member in question. With his dual identity of Michael at work and Michelle the rest of the time, I would imagine it would be difficult to remember which restroom and which mannerisms to use in such a lifestyle. After their initial shock, his peers treated him like anyone else, although he was well known at his base. That is the great thing about a flight attendant's world: Nothing is unheard of and normalcy is a fallacy.

Even though I was based overseas, I wondered if I would ever fly with him, as I was interested in hearing his story. One night, at a crew layover party I had a bit too much to drink. It had been a long time since I danced with Jack Daniels, but that was the drink of the day.

A crewmember pointed out an attractive girl across the room. "That's the Michael/Michelle girl you have always heard about," he whispered in my ear.

I peered anxiously at the other side of the room and saw an extremely attractive, albeit young, dark skinned lady sipping a glass of wine.

"No way, it couldn't be!" I was stunned and had to get a closer look. I attempted to sober up a bit and made my way over. Luckily, she was talking with someone in my crew, so small talk came easy.

"Hey, Frank, I want you to meet a friend of mine. Michaela, this is Frank."

"It's a pleasure to meet you," I shook her hand and could not believe that this young lady was really a man. I thought she went by Michelle but did not want to let on quite yet that I knew about her. Usually one can tell in those matters, but I couldn't find a trace of masculinity much less an Adam's apple. I had to be careful to avoid staring too much at her. She was lovely to talk to, and unfortunately I had more to drink. Her voice was soft and higher pitched than I expected. She was the best-looking and most convincing transvestite that I had ever seen. Okay granted, I have seen very few, but I was impressed nonetheless.

A group of us left to have a late night snack at the corner diner and luckily Michaela joined us. In talking with her I tried to allude to her personal situation, but could tell that she was unwilling to divulge anything remotely related to her deep secret. I didn't want to pry, but I was dead curious and wanted to write a story on her unique situation.

"Would I recognize you if I saw you in uniform?" I asked trying to be sly.

"Probably not, I look quite a bit different at work than I do now."

"So I have heard."

"So your wife works for us?" she blurted out, presumably thinking that I was hitting on her.

"Yes, she does." I took it as a hint to back off and stopped my staring.

I was merely flabbergasted at what an attractive woman she was. I wasn't interested in her in any sexual way but found her situation fascinating. Back at the hotel, we entered the elevator together and Michaela and I got off on the same floor. We made small talk on the way to our rooms. "I have had a difficult situation at home lately and haven't been able to smile, so tonight was a refreshing change," she said as she put the key in her door.

"Yeah, I have heard you know. And If I were you I would keep the penis, I have grown attached to mine," I said, trying to be cute and open-minded.

She smiled awkwardly at me and said good night. I decided her secret was a bit much to divulge to a stranger.

The next day on the flight back, the co-worker who introduced me to Michaela approached. "Did you have a bit too much to drink last night, Frank?"

"I may have. Why? Did I do something terrible?" I scrolled through the night's events in a panic.

"Well, I thought you were all right, but I talked to Michaela this morning and she told me that you started a conversation about your...uh...well, your penis?"

"No, it wasn't about my penis, it was about hers and her situation."

"What the hell are you talking about?"

"You know, the Michael/Michaela issue. Her being a guy and all."

She paused for a second, and her confused look turned into enlightenment and then transformed into laughter. "You think Michaela is a guy?"

"Well, yeah, isn't she?" I suddenly became embarrassed.

"No, you're thinking of Michelle and, while she was there briefly, she left early. Come to think of it, around the time you approached Michaela and me. She thought you were either hitting on her, giving her advice about her difficult boyfriend situation at home, or just a nut case."

I was guilty of the last offense and mortified. "I have grown attached to mine"? What an idiot I had been! I tried to convince her to keep quiet about the incident, but that, of course, did not happen. I ran into Michaela about a year later and after the eight shades of red and many apologies, we laughed about it.

I never ended up meeting Michael, but he now is officially and surgically Michelle. I hear she is still flying, married, and in the process of adopting a baby girl.

I never danced with Jack Daniels again.

Have a Heart

Linda was a normal run-of-the-mill flight attendant. She was 45 years old, with a pleasant, reserved personality, trying very hard not to stand out in the crowd. She never partied with the crew and rarely divulged personal information. So, when I received a phone call from her while on a San Francisco layover, I was more than a little astonished. I was the purser and forgot she was even on the crew.

"Frank, I just thought I would call and tell you that I won't be on the flight home."

"Why not? What's wrong?"

"Uh…well, I have to go to the hospital." She paused, trying not to cry. "They have a heart for me."

"What? I mean …I beg your pardon?"

"I have been on the transplant list for several years and, miraculously, it's my turn and they have a match. I rented a car and have a two-hour drive ahead of me so I had better be going. Wish me luck!" She hung up the phone.

"Good luck," I mumbled as I stared out the window in disbelief. The thought of Linda driving herself to the hospital for such a monumental procedure haunted the deepest part of me. Many of us have had relatives who have undergone a heart bypass or some type of heart surgery, but instead of cleaning out a pipe, it's like replacing the whole plumbing system. She was given only a 40% chance of survival with the operation, but this was better than the 2% without. The hardest part was getting the donor heart. Now, they had one.

I checked in with her progress and was pleased the operation went well. The memory of Linda faded with time. A couple of years later at a Pan Am reunion, I heard from some friends that the heart she received was from a 14 year old. Which would normally be good, but since she had always had a bad heart, her organs had been weakened due to bad circulation. When they put a strong heart in, it was a major shock to her system. Her prognosis wasn't good, but the operation gave her extra time to get her affairs in order.

Three years later, at the airport after a flight, a hand tapped me on the shoulder. It was a very different looking Linda in uniform. I didn't recognize her at first, but when I did, I was speechless. She was considerably thinner and looked like she had been through a lot. I thought she had died and had no idea she was still flying.

"Oh, my God," was all I could manage to say.

A stray tear limped off her big smile. "I made it."

"Can I hug you?" I asked cautiously.

"You'd better."

We talked for hours over coffee as she explained all that had happened. I was fascinated even though, as a bit of a hypochondriac, I am normally queasy at in-depth medical talk. She wasn't sure about what the future held, but she was just glad to be there. To say I remotely comprehended what she had been through would be a lie. Even though her exterior looked tired, I noticed the sparkle in her eyes as we talked — a sparkle that I had not seen in her before the operation.

While writing this story six years later, I looked up Linda's flight schedule to see if she was still flying. I am happy to report that she is based in Paris, still flying and happier than ever. I even have a message from her to all of you: "Don't take anything in life for granted, and please fill out your donor cards."

Good advice from a remarkable lady.

Terminal 3

Making the Frank Connection

A Day That Will Live in Infamy

I was a passenger flying to New York one early fall morning. I had a meeting with a publicist about my book launch which was due to take place in three days time. I was anxious to get there but fell asleep regardless.

Before landing, the captain made the following announcement:

"Ladies and gentlemen, there has been a serious accident on the ground and we are being ordered to divert to another airport and wait for further instructions. We will give you more information when it is given to us. This is not airline specific, but rather a nationwide order. At this time I am going to insist that no one leave their seats for any reason until we open the doors. Once on the ground you will be permitted to use your cell phones, but anyone who leaves their seat will be met by authorities."

Confusion hit the cabin as I noticed all the worried looks on the flight attendants' faces. They were trying to hide from the passengers and their questions. One flight attendant curiously clutched an ice mallet as if for self-defense. She had a frightened expression but never took her eyes off of the passengers.

All I could think about was the meeting that I was going to miss. We landed somewhere in Pennsylvania and were held at a remote location for 30 minutes. Many people tried their cell phones, but, due to a heavy volume, only a few calls were connected. The calls that did get through provided some factual information along with mild hysteria. The chatter of an airplane crashing into the World Trade Center, World War III, and the assassination attempt of the President circulated throughout the cabin.

We pulled up to a gate and the agent in tears announced, "There has been a national tragedy, commercial planes have struck certain buildings in America...." She continued to cry and was unable to say more.

I kept trying my cell phone, but all circuits were busy. We boarded a shuttle bus to take us to the main terminal. I started to get annoyed at a hysterical woman crying next to me. Everyone was so over-dramatic when it came to these things, I thought as I redialed my cell phone in frustration. I finally got through to my wife as she burst into floods of tears. All she knew was that I was scheduled to land in New York at 9:15 a.m., four passenger planes had crashed into buildings which had collapsed, thousands were dead, and I wasn't answering my cell phone. She was positive I had perished. Tears rushed to my eyes.

Inside the airport people gathered around a large-screen television and watched with disbelief. The rest is, as they say, history. Air travel suddenly ceased, a nation was in shock, thousands perished, and millions lost hope. America was the victim of the worst terrorist activity ever.

I was somewhere in Pennsylvania and didn't have a clue about what to do next. After two days of shock, I managed to carpool back to the West Coast with total strangers – a guy who chain-smoked, one who had an odor problem, and another who was a know-it-all on world affairs. I spent September 15th, the day of my scheduled book launch party, pretending I was asleep in the back of a car, feeling sorry for myself.

Unfortunate circumstances unfurled in my mind. My book had been released in bookstores the day before the tragedy; it was titled *The Air Travelers Survival Guide*; the cover showed a pilot parachuting out of an airplane window; the publisher's name was Impact; and I warned of terrorist activities in one of the chapters. Oh, my God, what had I done? This was a nightmare.

My depression deepened from my guilt of worrying about a silly book, when over five thousand people were presumed dead. I knew it was only human nature to relate tragedy to our own personal situation, but a vicious cycle of guilt was repeating in my head.

Taking four-hour shifts at the wheel, we drove across America. Do you know how boring it is on the roads between Chicago and Denver? You never quite appreciate air travel until you have to drive the distance. What normally took four hours by air took four days by car.

A curious thing happened as we started getting closer to California. People started flying the American flag from their cars. "God Bless America" graced every digital sign and tollbooth on the roads. Ray Charles's version of *America the Beautiful* played from every radio station. Patriotism was alive and thriving in America. From the back seat I saw everyone, from truck drivers to young children, wearing, waving, or honoring the stars and stripes in some way. I was amazed and suddenly had renewed pride in being an American.

I had thought of the old movie, Starman, where Jeff Bridges, as the alien, said, "You humans are a peculiar and beautiful race, for you are always at your best when the times are at their worst." How true to life is that?

I returned home, gave blood, and cried for the next two days. My wife was furloughed from her pilot job and we decided to tone down book publicity and promotions. I also decided to donate portions of the book proceeds to the "9/11 Families of Flight Attendant Victims Fund." So, to all of you who bought that book, part of your money has gone to a good cause.

As a nation, we are recovering slowly but will never forget. Go home tonight and hug your spouse, child, or pet a little tighter. You made it through a tough period; others were not as lucky. With the lines for blood donors, the amount of charity donations, and the millions of thoughtful gestures during this tragedy, I truly feel that America is indeed blessed.

Have a Seat

These days it seems you either need a shoehorn to squeeze into your Economy seat or a master's degree to decipher the First Class seat instruction manual.

The seat in general is a wonderful invention. It is a vehicle designed to take direct stress off of the knees, thus resting the lower extremities. The seat is best taken with moderate doses of television or a good book. With the evolution of the seat and the benefit of modern technology, you wonder how the airlines managed to perfect the art of making the seats in Economy more and more uncomfortable.

The airlines would like to hide the obvious fact that more seats equal more revenue. They live in a fantasy world where the normal passenger is 5 foot 6 inches tall and 160 pounds or less. Things get quite tricky when you are over 6 feet tall or carrying around some extra body weight. One airline's solution was to charge extra-large passengers more. In addition to the carry-on baggage template, maybe there will be a big-butt template? "Excuse me sir, could you please have a seat in the Dairy Air-o-Meter?" I imagine in the future there could be an airline designed for the overweight passengers. Wouldn't Richard Simmons be the perfect flight attendant for that airline?

In an attempt to make you forget how uncomfortable you are, the airlines stick a video screen in front of you. If the video system is actually working, it hopefully will keep your mind off of your throbbing knees and swelling feet. The only problem with this is that they put the outlet box under the seat in front of you, taking away even more of your precious foot space. Don't you just love the announcement upon boarding, "Your primary luggage stowage area is located under the seat in front of you."

Where? You have got to be kidding! Yes, we are. We don't actually believe it either, but have to make the announcement regardless.

You shimmy your way into the small seat and try to make the best of a tiny situation. You get accustomed to it after a while and try to fool yourself that it is not as bad as you had originally thought. The seatbelt sign goes off and the person in front of you reclines his seat into your lap. As you analyze the head that is now two inches from your face, your blood begins to boil. You feel this person is being rude and selfish. Did you know 75% of all in-flight fights are caused by disputes relating to the seat-reclining issue? People are very protective of their personal space no matter how small it may be. You decide to let the greedy seat occupant in front of you know about your discomfort, so you bump the seat. You decide to do it again, as they ignored the first hint. Believe me, they feel every bump. Two or three more times and you have the makings of a fight. Realize you can always negotiate the seat angle with the person in front of you. Don't kick the seat first, as the negotiation process will be considerably more difficult.

Whose fault is it? The person in front of you has a right to recline their seat as undoubtedly the passenger in front of them has done the same. You are entitled to your space no matter what ticket price you pay, so, to answer the question, it is the airline's fault, not the flight attendant's. During the meal service you can always ask the person in front of you to bring their seat up a little to avoid getting a Chicken Parmesan hairdo. Or ask a flight attendant to ask them to raise their seat, as they know of this problem all too well.

What about the little game of "Master of the Armrest"? It is a universal game played by all cultures around the world. You sit down and the person next to you has their arm covering the whole armrest. The moment they move it for any reason, you quickly slide your arm in, establishing your stake of ownership, and pretend to fall asleep. This goes back and forth for the remainder of the flight. Not a word is spoken about the game, but everyone is aware as it plays out. It's an armrest, for goodness sake! Many people forget that it's meant to be shared. Your elbow on one half and the other person's elbow on the other half. The most common problem is during the game the person in possession usually takes the whole thing. Everything in life can be negotiated, even the armrest.

A new airline scheme making its way to the front line is the different classes among classes. No longer is it just First, Business, and Economy, but here comes Economy First with an extra six inches of legroom and Economy Business with two inches. One airline even came out with the advertisement slogan of "What would you do with an extra six inches?" They scrapped the idea once they realized the sexual innuendo. Sexual innuendo? Really? I would have kept it as an eye grabber, but I guess that's why there isn't a Frank's Airline.

At the opposite end of the airplane are the seats resembling some kind of futuristic telepod. Each of these seats extend out into a full-length bed and has a VCR, desk, privacy barrier, a computer power outlet with an Internet connection, noise cancellation headsets, and even a back massager. Unless you are a frequent flyer, most of these amenities go unused because of the daunting instruction manual in the seat back pocket. I once had an older lady ask me with a terrified expression what the eject button was for. She was relieved when I explained that it was for the VCR and not the seat.

Do you think it's intentional that boarding is done from the front of the aircraft, displaying the deluxe seats you aren't sitting in? By the time you get to the Economy Coach Class, the seats look like the size of a shoebox.

Airlines do listen to the survey results, and unfortunately seat comfort ranks low in priority for most travelers who are concerned with On-Time Departure and Arrival. I prefer to believe this is in addition to safety. If you are not satisfied with your seat's comfort, don't yell at me – I do the serving, not the designing. I suggest you write it in on your next survey or, better yet, write a letter to customer service. Until then, the only advice I can offer is to ask at check-in for a seat in the front rows of the Economy section. The gate agent will know what you mean without you having to come out and say it.

I do think it is a bit absurd that people in Economy could be paying a wide range of prices for the same seat. Ideally, the new class scheme is designed to give the higher revenue passengers and the elite members of the frequent flyer program an added perk of a few inches of leg room. But what will end up happening is the clever traveler will get a $200 international round-trip ticket seated in Economy First, while another passenger paying $1,200 for the same trip is seated in Economy Coach.

My solution to this whole class within a class issue is that instead of six inches of extra leg room for a few rows, give two extra inches for the whole section. I even have the perfect ad slogan: "Two inches can make all the difference in the world."

Dancing to the Oldies

Oktoberfest in Munich, Germany can best be described as the World Series of beer or the Super Bowl of hops and barley. I was first introduced to this traditional festival when I played the trumpet in a band lucky enough to land a five-day gig in one of the beer tents. The German people look at the whole ordeal as somewhat of a tourist attraction, but I'll admit it, I'm a tourist. I have attended nine times since then, and every one of them was great.

Unfortunately, Munich trips are very senior, due to the flight hours, wonderful destination, and the specific aircraft. All of this means one thing: Don't even think about holding this trip unless you have over 35 years of seniority — and if it's around Oktoberfest time, 40. With my 14 years, I had no illusions about getting on the trip, but maybe I could talk one of the elders out of their flight and emphasize the benefit of free time. Begging eventually paid off and I was scheduled to work to Munich with a 30-hour layover, which was plenty of time to indulge.

The only problem was half the fun of a destination was whom you shared it with, and I was sure to either be alone or helping my fellow co-workers with their canes. I didn't care; I was going to enjoy the festival no matter what.

I entered the briefing room before the flight and it was as I had anticipated — gray hair, knitting needles, and not a familiar face among the crew. I made friendly and they smiled back wondering how I was able to be on the flight. It was then that I made my first mistake. A friend walked by the room and waved.

"Hey, Frank, where you going?" she asked.

"Munich for the Oktoberfest."

"You held those trips this month?"

I pointed to the lack of wrinkles around my eyes. "No way," I replied, trying to be cute. Then I realized I had said it in front of the very people I was ridiculing.

I froze with fear as I looked around to the now disapproving crew. Some asked what I had meant, others folded their arms and scowled, and one even stopped her knitting. Not a good way to start a European trip. I tried to play it off as a joke, but few, if any, found it amusing.

The flight went well and even though I expected the worst, the majority of the crew was fun to work with. On the bus to the hotel, Edith, the purser, turned to me and asked if I was interested in going to the beer fest with them. A part of me wanted to do it alone in search of a younger crowd, but the other part realized that if they were a drag I could always sneak out the back door.

"Sure, you all fancy a beer, do you?"

Everyone chuckled as Clay, the oldest male flight attendant I had ever seen, replied, "Son, I will drink you under the table."

Now, obviously he didn't realize whom he was dealing with, but it was a good sign that he was willing to try.

We met up after a short nap and even the cockpit crew joined us. I was still a bit groggy due to lack of sleep, but everyone else was chatty and in good spirits. Maybe it wasn't going to be as bad as I had originally feared.

We arrived at the festival grounds as I gazed with amazement at the multitude of people and events. My mouth began to water at the sight of the beer tents. Edith pointed out some of the attractions of interest and the plan of action. These people really had it going on, I thought. Her last comment of "be careful, as the beer here is stronger than the average German beer" had me assuming that they would probably be sipping colas all night.

I soon found out the opposite was true as they ordered beers left and right. We went from tent to tent, drinking, eating snacks, and enjoying ourselves. I hate to admit it, but I was having trouble keeping up with Clay, as he kept ordering rounds but showed no signs of the alcohol's effects. The night progressed joyously. I was going to teach the group the drinking songs, but not only did they know all of them, they also knew the associated dances and proceeded to perform them on top of the tables.

The variety of songs was amazing, from traditional German polkas to American country and western. And if you're wondering whatever happened to John Denver's music, it is still very much alive, as thousands of patrons from all over the world and I, oddly enough, screamed out several renditions of Country Roads and Rocky Mountain High.

We did everything from the chicken dance to the numerous toasting songs of Ein Prosit. And for anyone who has
attended the gala event, I have but one question: Who is
Alice anyway?

This was the hippest older crew I had ever flown with.
We sang with heart, drank arm in arm, and swayed back
and forth with the other tables. I was having the greatest
time when, all of a sudden, something peculiar started happening. Something so unheard of that I didn't want to admit it. I was getting drunk. I started slurring my speech
and my actions.

Let's face it, most of the people who go to the Oktoberfest
drink and eventually get drunk, but I was the only one
from my group who was starting to show. Clay kept ordering the rounds, dancing on the tables, and was completely in control of his actions. I wasn't, and I think some
of my crew realized it as well. I still danced and sang but
with caution and a glassy look to my eyes. The thing that
was so inconceivable to me was that I hadn't drunk any
more than the rest of my crew, but they were fine. Was I
out of shape? Could I have turned into a lightweight?

I awoke the next morning in the hotel room with my
head pounding, tongue feeling like a dry sponge, and no
recollection of how I got back to my room. I scrolled through
the night's events and remembered blurry interludes,
checked my wallet, and noticed I was alone, so all in all I
was in fairly good shape. Before pick-up from the hotel,
every crewmember called to see if I was all right, which
was not a good sign. The last thing I remembered was doing the chicken dance with Clay and then waking up in
my room. The crew would have to fill me in later.

My hangover settled in on the bus to the airport. But

even more degrading was the fact that everyone else was perky, in good humor, and showed no signs of a hangover. I started to turn green, and it wasn't from envy. The ladies told me that I had been fine towards the end of the evening but a little reserved. I hadn't said much, but when I did, it hadn't made much sense. Alberta and Edith had found me passed out in front of my hotel room door. I had the key in my hand but was apparently unable to make it work, so they had helped me.

"Wait a minute, I woke up in my underwear."

"Yes, we helped you with that as well...Oh, please, we have grandchildren older than you. But I must say that you are quite fit." Alberta winked at me.

"Thanks, I think." I felt greener and prayed for the bus ride to end.

Now, working a full trip with a hangover is an experience to avoid at all costs. I ended up paying for my indiscretions as the flight hours slowly ticked away. It wouldn't have been so bad if at least one person had joined me in my misery. I had no such luck, as these people were bubbly and full of spunk and vigor. I was the killjoy of the group, dreaming of my bed that awaited me at the end of the journey.

When the flight ended, I thanked everyone for a memorable time. I bowed to Clay and stated that I was not worthy and hightailed it home for a long, long slumber. I had a great time, but realized that I had done myself a great disservice by making assumptions about the actions of others. I wouldn't have had half the fun if I'd ventured out alone, and who knows what shape I would have turned up in. At the end of the day, don't judge a book by its cover, no matter how worn the cover is.

Wings of Flight

It was a typical summer day rush hour at the airport. The gate agents were trying to get the flight out before the thunderstorm hit. This hope was suddenly dashed with the bright flashes of lightning, signaling a long delay. The flight attendants and pilots went on board but the gate agents held off passenger boarding until a new departure time was established. This time was different for me, as I was a passenger on my way to my grandmother's funeral.

 The new departure time was announced and much to everyone's disappointment, it meant a four-hour delay. The air conditioning in the gate area was broken, and the storm became fierce. It was hot and sticky, children were screaming, and people became irritable. I sat back and pondered global overpopulation. Which was a bit odd considering the sad event I was attending. I hated funerals; they were usually full of false emotions, sad thoughts and many times left the attendees with an unhappy aftertaste. I would rather say good-bye on my own terms, holding onto positive recollections.

Two unbearably long hours into the delay I was on the verge of reconsidering my trip and leaving. A silence hit as a small bluebird flew in and landed on the window ledge. All eyes were on the beautiful bird as our new guest served as a peaceful distraction. It flew from ledge to ledge singing a little song at every stop. It was as if it was sent to cheer us up, though it was probably just trying to stay out of the rain.

Fifteen minutes later, a uniformed man armed with a small net arrived. He had undoubtedly been instructed to remove our new-found friend. A few boos and hisses sounded in the background as the man made several attempts but missed. Every time he got close, the bird would fly to the other side of the gate area. The bird knew to stay well away. A curious thing happened — we all started cheering for the bluebird. The man would take a swipe with the net and when the bird flew to the other side, cheers rang out from everyone. This continued for about ten minutes while the uniformed man became more disheartened with each cheer.

He stopped and approached the microphone and announced, "Ladies and gentlemen, you don't seem to understand. I am an employee on my off time. I am trying to catch this bird, because if I don't, they will be exterminating it tonight. I am only trying to save it."

Everyone looked around at each other a bit ashamed as he went back to the task at hand. This time the cheers were for the man, as a form of crowd participation began. When the bird flew away, the people on the other side would stand up and cheer, attempting to scare the bird back to the man holding the net. It was as if we were at a baseball game performing the Mexican wave. A collective shout rang out from all sides. Everyone, including myself, was getting into the spirit. Passengers from other gates crowded around and marveled at the spectacle.

The team effort continued for around 20 minutes until one successful swipe of the net caught the bird. Thunderous applause broke out; people hugged and congratulated each other on a job well done. The man walked to the nearest window, opened it and let our friend loose. Everyone gathered around the window as we watched the bluebird fly off.

"Ladies and gentlemen, we are now ready to board this flight..." the gate agent announced.

Another round of applause rang out. Never in my whole flying career have I seen passengers as happy and courteous at the end of a four-hour delay. Sometimes, even in the worst of times, all we need in life is a small distraction to restore a sense of humanity in all of us.

During the funeral I spotted a bluebird and smiled. I believe my Granny would have wanted it that way.

Picture This

On a flight to Amsterdam, Kristy, a cute but shy flight attendant, thought she knew my wife but asked to see a picture just in case. When I pulled out a little travel photo album she smiled and replied that she had one of her family as well. We exchanged albums as the call button went off. She held up her hand and said it was her turn and ventured up the aisle. I stood in the galley and turned the first page of her photographs. I was amazed when the first few pictures showed this lovely girl and her husband in slinky lingerie. Maybe she wasn't as shy as I had initially suspected. I was shocked when the next few pictures were of them naked and in compromising positions. By the third page it was becoming clear to me that Kristy accidentally gave me the wrong photo album.

I looked up the aisle and she was nowhere to be seen. Being only human, I slipped back into the galley and flipped quickly through the pictures. There were various sexual positions, costumes, and close-ups that made me blush and feel guilty for turning the pages.

I shut the album quickly when she returned and with a shy grin remarked, "You really didn't mean to give me this photo album, did you?"

"Why, what do you mean?" She looked down at the cover and in an instant her face lost all color. Her knees buckled slightly but she was able to grab the book from my hands. She appeared to be on the verge of fainting.

"Oh, my God! I am so sorry! You didn't look at all the pictures, did you?"

"No, don't worry about it. I just turned the first page and realized that you might have made a mistake."

She took solace in my statement but was extremely shy around me the remainder of the flight. On the layover, the rest of the crew were slam-clicks, not interested in going out, so Kristy and I agreed to meet up for a drink at the hotel bar after a nap.

We had a few beers, loosened up, and exchanged flight stories for a while. The conversation got interesting when she mentioned the photo album.

"I can't believe I gave you the wrong album. I am still embarrassed."

"Now that you mentioned it, how did you get some of those pictures developed?" I said with a grin.

"I knew you saw more than you let on. Oh well, serves me right!" She smiled and ordered another round.

"How did you get into some of those positions? With a timer?"

The laughter became quite heavy and even though Kristy's face was beetroot red, she could appreciate the humor involved.

"No, but, seriously, why would you carry those around?" I asked.

"Well, I am a newlywed and my husband works for weeks at a time out on the ocean. Sometimes it can be a whole month before we are together. This way we have something to remind us on the longer stretches, if you know what I mean."

I told her while I could appreciate what she was saying, US Customs would not and therefore consider it pornography. "They will consider the pictures illegal and will confiscate them. You know very well that before the pictures are filed away, every Customs agent and their friends are bound to get an eyeful, if not a copy."

Folks, I don't care if it's innocent or not. Pornography and traveling don't mix. My main advice is to keep anything remotely risqué at home. Nudity is not considered porn but anything including another person, marital aid, or animal, is, and can be construed as X-rated. So in this case, porn is in the eye of the Customs agent. It's not worth the embarrassment or label of porn smuggler. Don't buy that video or CD-ROM in Amsterdam and leave your naughty partner pics at home.

Or, as my wife puts it, "Take a mental picture."

The Travel Stink Factor

How many times have you been on an airplane and were suddenly blindsided by an overpowering smell, good or bad? From the occasional engine exhaust to the other people on the plane, odors thrive and sometimes get the better of you in-flight. Most bad smells are tolerable for the shorter flights, but if you are next to someone who burns your nose hair every time they speak and the flight is to last an hour or more, you may have a problem. The following is a closer look into the common smells you might encounter on a flight and some possible solutions for clearing the air.

Breath — Now, as someone who talks to many people, I can speak with a little authority on this matter. I enjoy garlic, onions, and spicy foods; if it makes your breath sour I usually like it. I have been the culprit in many odoriferous conversations. An ex-girlfriend even told me in mid-sentence that if I spoke one more word she would faint. I got the hint but there are nicer ways about this. Fresh breath isn't really noticeable but stale breath is, and bad breath can be downright paralyzing. How many times have you been on an airplane and a person five rows back yawns and makes you feel like ripping off your nose? There are plenty of excuses for halitosis from tooth abscesses to alcoholism, but bad breath is bad breath, regardless.

My advice is:

1. Bring a toothbrush on longer flights and brush every time you use the lavatory.

2. Bring breath mints or chewing gum.

3. Watch out for the obvious signs such as: People talking to you but breathing from the side of their mouths, the unmistakable scowl from others, or you breathe deeply and the person next to you passes out.

4. Give and get the hint. If anyone offers you a mint take it. Nine out of ten times they are dropping you a hint. Offer offenders a mint and be persistent. If they decline, tell them that they really need it. I know I would want to know.

Feet — This is when you've got way too much sole. These days, we are realizing that a shoe can be used as a deadly weapon, but here I am talking about the actual foot as the ammunition. If you suffer from the old curse of stink foot, an airplane is not the place to shed those vessels around your feet. I worked a flight where I could have sworn the person who removed his shoes must have backpacked across the entire Himalayan mountain range without washing his feet. The smell was beyond description. When people started to get physically sick and he declined to put his shoes back on, we had to get the captain to threaten police action. He eventually complied. A fallacy many share is that bad foot odors dissipate with time. False. For you maybe, but not the dozens forced to sit around you. Be kind to your neighbors. You know whether your feet stink or not; if you can smell your own feet, multiply it by ten and this is what everyone else smells.

I flew with a group of runners who had just completed the London Marathon and instead of a smelly foot cloud I received a lesson in Foot Smell 101. If you have to take off your shoes, go to the lavatory, change your socks, and place your shoes and old socks in a plastic bag. Never walk around the airplane barefoot, especially in the toilet vicinity, because even Frank's aim is occasionally bad.

The Pits — If you have ever been on a full 747 flight to India, then you have undoubtedly been hit with the sharp blast of body odor. Unfortunately, this may be difficult to avoid when traveling to destinations where antiperspirants are not a widely used commodity. But for those of us who aren't from non Third-World countries, there is no excuse for the extreme cases of body odor; I don't care how hot it is. Sometimes there are shower facilities at airports, gift shops with deodorants, and even clothing stores. The best advice I can give to someone who is trapped next to stinky pits is to put a dab of lotion with your favorite scent under each nostril. Every smell is transformed into a pleasant one. On the flights to India the flight attendants would share and compare lotions. Most effective scent was lavender by far. We had the softest upper lips around.

Perfumes and colognes — Now, saying all of this about body odor leads me to the other side of the spectrum. Too much of a good thing can actually be a bad thing. Americans are so afraid of body odor that they tend to overdo it a bit and pile on the perfume. Remember, one man's cologne is another man's skunk juice. It is only natural the body emits odors; the key is not having the odor overpower or offend. Have you ever been in an elevator and couldn't stand someone's perfume? Multiply it by 200 and by the amount of hours on your flight, and you have a cacophony of smells. Most people like smelling nice, but all that is needed is one squirt instead of your traditional three or four. As the slogan goes, a little dab will do ya.

Nail her — The practice of doing your nails onboard should be forbidden. It is forbidden on some but unfortunately not my airline. It's selfish, inconsiderate, and sometimes dangerous. It is as rude as smoking in an elevator or passing gas in someone's face. The smell from the nail polish is the fastest spreading agent onboard. If a passenger in First Class does her nails, it is not unheard of to smell the scent of polish in the last row of Economy. The reason for this is that the filters in the oxygen system are unable to filter out the odoriferous element in nail polish. If you witness or are exposed to someone on the plane doing their nails, notify a flight attendant. I know most flight attendants will forbid it; I know I would.

There once was a passenger who refused when told to stop her lengthy nail procedure because it was causing people to become ill. She was met by authorities and booked on disobeying an in-flight directive. When she attempted to sue the airlines, the judge fined her $10,000 in wasted legal costs. Now that settles well in my mind.

Aircraft odors — Upon pushback from the gate, sometimes you smell exhaust. While annoying, this is nothing to get scared about. This is usually due to the airplane's oxygen system still operating on ground mode. When the engines start up on some of the older planes, exhaust is sucked inside. But I must add that whenever you smell smoke, see smoke, or think you smell or see smoke, notify the nearest crewmember immediately. Many times, it's the passengers who notice smoke first. They fail to notify the crew, mistakenly assuming they are already aware of the situation. Every second counts with an emergency of this nature. Did you know the biggest danger onboard an aircraft is fire?

To Air is Human — This leads me to the body's true whoopee cushion. I was told to avoid this personal subject as it is something that should be recognized but not spoken of unless in jest. Well, along with being Frank comes great responsibility and considering this is one of Frank's areas of expertise, I would be remiss in my duties to refrain. Cutting the cheese, spliffing, farting, seeing the man about some methane, whatever you want to call it, everyone has it in common, but, and I do mean butt, some more than others. When it comes to boarding an airplane though, things can get tricky.

You've been to a foreign destination. Your diet and nutrition table went out the window and you decided to try new cuisine. You tried yeast beer in Germany, tasted a new recipe for cabbage, or maybe you merely descended from a genetically airy family. Whatever the excuse, air travel doesn't mean the same as traveling with air. There are ways of dealing with these situations effectively and others to avoid. In my earlier book I defined the art of crop dusting as walking up the aisle and passing gas. It may have sounded as if it was a practice I condoned; it was merely stating a reality for both passengers and crew. The best suggestion I can give is to let the lavatories do their magic. Merely sit down, do your thing and flush at the same time. The massive air suction that the toilet provides is ample to eradicate any amount of brussels sprouts. The other piece of advice is that if you are prone to such outbursts, than bring along some neutralizing medication.

Frank's recommendation is GasX. Another hint is if you know that you shouldn't be eating something and you are within hours of air travel, simply put, don't. The air pressure up in the sky matched with the building air pressure inside your body is no fight you want to pick; you will lose and so will everyone else around you.

I was a First Class passenger on a flight where we had a mystery gasser. It got so bad that most everyone had to stuff tissues up their noses. Most passengers assumed it was from a 300-pound man snoring away in the corner, but when it got so bad a flight attendant went way beyond the call of duty and did some nostril investigation. She was able to determine that the offender was a well-dressed business-man on the other side of the cabin. She questioned him, and when he finally came clean, his excuse was, "I am sorry, I just couldn't help it." Meanwhile the restroom was never occupied and nothing impeded his utilizing the facilities. The flight attendant paused a second and then responded,

"I have a small piece of advice for you sir, next time, CLENCH!" Applause rang through the cabin, and the businessman caught the hint.

So in the words of a wise flight attendant, utilize the appropriate facilities or "CLENCH!"

Chapter 11

No, I don't mean the chapter after ten and the one before twelve; the subject I am speaking of is the dreaded Chapter 11 bankruptcy protection. This is when a company can no longer contain its losses and profitability seems a remote future hope. The company throws itself at the mercy of the bankruptcy court and asks permission to break its promises to lenders, clients, and employees, in order to survive. In the process, many lives are turned upside down. Uncertainty, panic, and fear prevail as the future changes forever. It appears that Chapter 11 is a trend among most airlines these days, and the light at the end of the tunnel gets farther and farther away. I am no stranger to Chapter 11, as my former airline went down and eventually out, on this very road. The final three nails in Pan Am's coffin were bad management, the Lockerbie tragedy, and the Gulf War. Coincidently, many of the airlines today are suffering from bad management, the 9/11 tragedy, and yet another Gulf war. It's like a bad case of deja vu, all over again. Every now and then, I pass a fellow Pan Am friend and all that needs to be said is, "Here we go again," smile, and then walk on.

Many people invest their lives, money, and thoughts in their company. They go through record earnings, healthy retirement accounts, well-funded pension plans, etc., only to turn the economic corner and find themselves and their company in the midst of financial ruins.

While no company "enjoys" Chapter 11, it does give the company the opportunity to destroy in minutes what took the unions years to accomplish. Fair work rules, adequate compensation, and basic common decency are but a few items that get slashed. Chapter 11 is not the real danger, as it is only the re-organization period — relief from all the creditors, if you will. The real danger is Chapter 7 — liquidation of assets, the closing of doors, the death of the company. When Pan Am closed the doors, it was swift, precise, and sudden. Even though it took 20 years to bring the once prestigious airline down, the final days happened so quickly that a friend of mine was on a layover in South America the last day of Pan Am. She woke up, turned on CNN, and learned about the cessation of all operations. She received no phone call, message, or any communication from the company, which was strange because the crews' pick-up for the return flight was just one hour away. Sure enough, when the crew convened, Pan Am was no more, and what followed was a form of sky hitchhiking to get back home. The other airlines felt pity and accommodated most down-line employees, but some crews took over a week to get back. Could you imagine worrying about getting home when you have no airline or career left to return to? I heard of one person who was enormously in debt and had nothing or no one to return to, so he didn't. He just stayed in the country where he was when he discovered he no longer had a job.

The problem is that when you are in the flight attendant line of work and have around 10 years to go until retirement, you can't start over, don't have enough money to retire, and aren't really employable, having only the technical experience of a waiter. One flight attendant whom I fly with has been through seven airlines. Seven times she has been furloughed, made redundant, or the airline shut down. She is 56 years old and well prepared to go to another airline. I have started over once, and I can tell you, never again. Most flight attendants said that with Pan Am, but I see many of them in the airports from time to time.

Faced with Chapter 11, some employees run around in panic, acting as if the sky was falling and the end of the world was imminent. Others take advantage of everything they can, pilfering, using excessive sick leaves, etc., and others act as if it's a normal occurrence. I used to be one of the panic-strikers, asking the constant question "what if," until a wise old friend remarked, "If my aunt had a moustache, she'd be my uncle." At first, I laughed because he didn't know my aunt, but she did have her fair share of facial hair. I then thought about it and it made a lot of sense. "What ifs" aren't worth dwelling on; they only fester in the mind, create havoc, and eventually play out worse than reality.

If, as a passenger, you fly on an airline currently in Chapter 11, it is best to pay with a credit card. This way you can get a full and quick refund if something happens. As a courtesy, don't query the flight attendants about what will happen to your frequent flyer points should the airline cease operations. They are worried about more important things — their mortgage, kids, debts, etc. Instead call the customer service of the frequent flyer program; they are well prepared for these types of queries. Also try to be kind to the airline workers; even when things go wrong, your statement of "No wonder you're going out of business" hurts more than you can imagine.

To all of the workers currently going through, or who have gone through, the turmoil of Chapter 11 and/or Chapter 7, I wish you the best. I am with you. I really mean it, I am with you. Hope for the best, but prepare for the worst. Good luck and may God bless.

I try not to worry about it too much, as this would be merely another chapter in my life.

The Good Air

My jubilation at a layover in Buenos Aires was somewhat dampened by my airline's announcement of filing bankruptcy protection the day before the trip. Many employees would face an uncertain future, work rules would be tougher, and the impact on our wallets was sure to follow. At a time in my life when I should have been getting promotions and bonuses, I was maxed out in raises and taking pay cuts instead. My rationale for being in this job was starting to fade and harder to explain to the in-laws.

I wasn't going to let the news spoil my adventure. I had never been to Argentina before, and world discovery was at the top of my job rationale list. The East Coast had just been hit with a massive snowstorm and my destination's hot summer conditions made the trip more enticing. The weather was perfect, the people friendly, and the hotel was fancy. The exchange rate was amazing so, even though I had to start minimizing expenses, I rationalized I was saving money by spending more. I love how the brain works. I explored the city, observed the people, wrote in the local park, and worked out in the hotel gym. Sounds disciplined? Well, to be honest I mostly sunbathed by the pool and sipped margaritas. There is something quite decadent about soaking in the sun while your neighbors back home are under a foot of snow. My job satisfaction was slowly returning.

The crew boarded the return flight rejuvenated and slightly sunburnt. The gate agent informed us that most of our passengers were from the Annual World Special Olympics. There were 21 wheelchairs users and many others with disabilities. We pre-boarded those needing special help, which was most of our passengers. The jetway was lined with wheelchairs, little people, seeing-eye dogs, people with mental retardation, etc. We did our best to help in any way we could.

The only hitch occurred when the pilots boarded. The captain made the unfortunate statement of "It's like a freaking circus in here." Now, I have a great respect for airline pilots and a good understanding of the extent of their training, but a majority of them should not be allowed to speak in public. The greeter and I pretended not to notice, but unfortunately some of the chaperones overheard.

It was a tough flight but we managed just fine. Everyone from the group was very friendly and quite well behaved. One young lady in particular stood out. Her name was Sarah. She had a wonderful smile and always engaged me in friendly conversation as I passed. She had difficulty walking on her own, her eyes wouldn't open fully, and she had limited use of her arms. What impressed me most was her happy demeanor and positive outlook.

After the service, the crew gathered in the back galley and commiserated over the gloom and doom of our airline's financial situation. People began to ask themselves the "what ifs" and "what will I do?" I am normally the optimist and comedian in these situations, but I had serious doubts as well. I had lived my life on my terms, avoided the daily traffic grind and office mentality, but most of all I was living the goal of not becoming like my father. I had not secured anything in my writing career and hadn't used my computer degree since the language COBOL was in use. So I joined in on the fear-and-misery meeting.

One older flight attendant, Karen, was on the verge of tears, explaining how the airline was her life and she had no savings or back-up plans. She was in deep distress. At which point Sarah appeared in the galley. She had gone to great lengths walking back unassisted for a glass of water. I rushed over, "You shouldn't have gotten up. That's what the call bell is for," a sentence that very rarely leaves my mouth.

"That's okay, I needed to stretch and get out of my seat anyway," she replied. She thanked us for the excellent service, told us of her adventures, and remarked how excited she was to get back to experience the new snow at home. She was bubbly and had a wonderful way about her. Everyone in the misery meeting listened and smiled.

"How do you do it? I mean, what makes you so happy and alive?" Karen asked in awe.

"Oh, I don't know, it's hard to complain about life when you are just thankful for the breath in your lungs." And so was the advice from a remarkable young lady who will always have difficulties in everything she attempts in life. Karen tried unsuccessfully to hold back her tears and hugged

Sarah for several minutes. There ended our meeting of despair and thus began a profound and warm moment of silence.

As the airline turmoil increases and the gloom grows even darker, it always helps me to think back on Sarah and thank life for the air in my lungs.

To the U.S. Special Olympic Team and Sarah, this one is for you and thank you for the breath of fresh air.

The Discount Epidemic

The low-cost, no-frills airlines are taking hold of the travel industry. All of the major carriers are now revamping their product to avoid loss of their regular customers. The discount airline's bottom line is to offer low-priced travel to a certain destination, without all the bells and whistles. Most of the time it's cattle car type service and the passenger ends up feeling like a number, but they pay a fraction of the normal cost.

What I find so incomprehensible is that the managers of the full-service airlines have been caught so way off guard. Why did they think this concept was certain to fail?

Let's see… Cheap tickets, increased frequency, little or no ridiculous penalties or restrictions? It sounds to me like it would work. Well, it has, and the growing forces of the no-frills airlines are eating into the major airlines' profits and intensifying their losses. I see it like the concept of the full-service gas pumps as opposed to self-service. How many people go to the full service? While there are still a few who do, the masses generally flock to the do-it-yourself-and-for-cheaper mode.

So, on your next flight you might have to take a sandwich, or get treated a little more rudely. At least you don't feel slammed by some silly restriction and you have saved a great deal of money in the process. I was floored when recently a friend bought a full fare ticket to Europe for a mere $185, but then a week later was obliged to book a trip only 400 miles away costing him $500. He couldn't go to another airline because no other airline could meet his itinerary needs. This is where the low-cost carriers are starting to come in and make the "big guys" accountable.

The following is a well-known story that puts all of this into perspective:

If the Airlines Sold Paint

Customer: Hi. How much is your paint?

Agent: Well, sir, that depends on quite a lot of things.

Customer: Can you give me a guess? Is there an average price?

Agent: Our lowest price is $15 a gallon, and we have 50 different prices up to $250 a gallon.

Customer: What's the difference in paint?

Agent: Oh, there isn't any difference; it's all the same.

Customer: Well, then I'd like some of the $15 paint.

Agent: When do you intend to paint?

Customer: I want to paint tomorrow; it's my day off.

Agent: Sir, the paint for tomorrow is the $250 paint.

Customer: When would I have to paint to get the $15 paint?

Agent: You would have to start very late at night in about two weeks. But you will have to agree to start painting before Friday of that week and continue painting until at least Sunday.

Customer: You have got to be kidding!

Agent: I'll check to see if we have any paint available.

Customer: You have shelves full of paint! I can see it!

Agent: But that doesn't mean that we have paint available. We sell only a certain number on any given weekend. Oh, and by the way, the price per gallon just went to $18. We don't have any more $15 paint.

Customer: The price went up as we were talking?

Agent: Yes, sir. We change the prices and rules hundreds of times a day, and since you haven't actually walked out of the store with your paint yet, we just decided to change. I suggest you purchase your paint as soon as possible. How many gallons do you want?

Customer: Well, maybe five gallons. Make it six, so I'll have enough.

Agent: Oh, no, sir, you can't do that. If you buy paint and don't use it, there are penalties and possible confiscation of the paint you already have.

Customer: WHAT?

Agent: We can sell enough paint to do your kitchen, bathroom, hall and north bedroom, but if you stop painting before you do the bedroom, you will lose your remaining gallons of paint.

Customer: What does it matter whether I use all the paint? I already paid you for it!

Agent: We make plans based upon the idea that all our paint is used, every drop. If you don't, it causes us all sorts of problems.

Customer: This is crazy! I suppose something terrible happens if I don't keep painting until after Saturday night?

Agent: Oh yes! Every gallon you bought automatically becomes the $250 paint.

Customer: But what are all these "Paint on sale from $12 a gallon" signs?

Agent: Well that's for our budget paint. It only comes in half-gallons. One $6 half-gallon will do half a room. The second half-gallon to complete the room is $20. None of the cans have labels, some are empty, and there are no refunds, even on the empty cans.

Customer: To hell with this! I'll buy what I need somewhere else!

Agent: I don't think so, sir. You may be able to buy paint for your bathroom and bedrooms, and your kitchen and dining room from someone else, but you won't be able to paint your connecting hall and stairway from anyone but us. And I should point out, sir, that if you paint in only one direction, it will be $350 a gallon.

Customer: I thought your most expensive paint was $250?

Agent: That's if you paint around the room and back to the point at which you started. A hallway is different.

Customer: And if I buy $250 paint for the hall, but only paint in one direction, you'll confiscate the remaining paint.

Agent: No, we'll charge you an extra usage fee plus the difference on your next gallon of paint. But I believe you're getting it now, sir.

Customer: You're insane!

Agent: Thanks for painting with us!

In the airline world, a new kind of paint store is revolutionizing the way people paint. If the big carriers don't catch on in time, it could make the world of paint...thinner.

Endless Summer

My firm belief is that out of lemons can come lemonade and every cloud does have a silver lining. Sometimes the silver lining is hard to find even if it stares you straight in the eyes, day in and day out.

Rick and Fred were flight attendants and long-time best friends. They were in their thirties and both lacked direction or purpose in life. They had joined the flight attendant ranks as a way of surfing around the world and meeting "babes," as they put it. Unfortunately, somewhere along the way they traded in their wetsuits and surfboards for three-piece suits and suitcases. They had become what they had always feared — responsible individuals. They never got to surf around the world seeking the answer to all life's questions in the "almighty wave." I had always wondered whatever happened to the carefree types in college. I guess even they grow up eventually, though secretly you hoped they wouldn't.

Rick was going through a messy divorce and Fred was in a failing real estate venture. The September 11th tragedy occurred and the airlines warned that hard times were definitely ahead. Misery loves company and all flight crews shared in the underlying depression.

We all got together at a pub on a London layover and decided to wash the blues away with beer. We discussed the layoffs and furlough programs occurring at work. Our airline was offering voluntary furloughs to flight attendants in order to prevent laying off surplus employees. The package included free travel benefits, medical and dental coverage, and no loss of seniority for up to two years. We all scrolled through the possibilities and ended with "If only we could."

It was as if a light bulb went off in Rick's head and then in Fred's.

"Why can't we?" asked Rick.

"Why can't we what?" Fred replied.

"Take the year off and have an endless summer. Do the things we wanted to do in the first place."

Fred started to grin. "Your divorce should be final and my grandfather did just leave me 50 thousand bucks in his will. I am sure he would have wanted it to go to a good cause."

"Are you guys being serious?" I asked with envious skepticism.

"Hell, yeah, why not?"they both replied with high fives and huge smiles.

The beer flowed faster and the talk grew wilder as ideas of traveling the world, surfing, snowboarding, and "really" living remained the only topic. Every ten minutes one of them would say, "Dude, I am really serious about this!" And the other would reply, "So am I!"

We stumbled back to the hotel. I drifted off to sleep and fantasized about what taking a year off from work would be like. I was excited for them but realized that it probably was the beer talking, as a follow-through would not likely be a reality.

A month later the voluntary furloughs were posted and under the two-year category were Fred's and Rick's names. So, not only did they go through with it, they doubled the initial intended length. Part of me jumped with excitement as if I were going with them. My wife and I had our fingers into too many projects at the moment to even consider it, but I was very happy for them.

How many of us dream of being free from all of our current responsibilities? Taking off for a year or two and discovering what life is really all about? Enjoying the world before having to worry about the foibles of old age and retirement funds? How many of us will get that chance? My cousin is a lawyer and hates her job. She and her husband are in the process of picking up stakes and exploring the world, planning never to return to the executive legal lifestyle. While this idea may scare many, it intrigues some. We had a going away BBQ for Rick and Fred, who were set to leave the next day for their first stop, the winter surf of Costa Rica. From there they were to go to the North Shore of Hawaii and then on to Australia, New Zealand, Thailand, Viet Nam, Russia, and Europe, after which they would play it by ear.

We had made an agreement that I would meet up with them from time to time and bring certain necessities from home. In return, I would get to play in their responsibility-free world for a short visit. My only stipulation was that wherever they went, they were to send a letter or postcard telling me briefly of their journeys. I have a map on the wall of my study with colored thumbtacks keeping track of their progress. I told them before they left they should take notes and we could write a book when they returned. They liked the idea and even suggested the title, "Rick and Fred's Excellent Adventure."

As this book was going to press, Fred and Rick were in New Zealand bungee jumping and surfing up a storm. I wish them well and plan to meet up with them in Thailand.

Their last postcard at the end read, "Say hello to reality for us!"

So here it goes, *"Hello, reality!"*

Terminal 4

Hooked On In-Flight

Addictive Personality

In life they say that there are two sure things — death and taxes. In the flying industry, the third sure thing is drug testing. It's the one test you can't study for, cheat on, or avoid. It's where one moment you feel like an individual and the next, a number, instructed to fill up a cup. Afterwards, if you hear nothing from the company, you passed. Where does your specimen go? What if the lab makes a mistake? Can inhaling second-hand marijuana smoke give a positive reading? All these questions, and more, pass through my mind each time I am tested. I have been tested on average twice annually for the past 18 years.

I remember being flagged in New York for a random drug test, along with an older flight attendant named Carol. She was about 68, a bit frail, and had a kind smile. She hadn't been tested for over 15 years, so I took her under my wing, stating that I was an "expert." I described the procedure, forms she had to sign, and ways to move things along faster. We both finished fairly quickly and caught a taxi to our layover hotel. In the cab she seemed a bit nervous.

"Frank, how well do you know the specifics of this type of testing?" she asked

"I am from California and used to be a surfer, so I guess you could say pretty well. Why?"

"Can you keep a secret?" she asked. I nodded my head suspiciously as she continued. "I smoked a joint with my girlfriend about three weeks ago. It was the first time in 20 years, but now I am scared to death."

My mouth nearly hit the floor. This lady was like my grandmother. I just couldn't imagine her smoking marijuana. Even though I was stunned, I tried to reassure her. I told her that if she wasn't a habitual user and it was only a small amount, it probably wouldn't affect the test result.

"Don't look so shocked. I was pretty crazy in my heyday. My friend is a glaucoma patient, so it was all legal... well, mostly." We laughed and let it go at that.

The airline insists that it is a random test, but one year I was tested nine times. By that time, I would have expected my urine to be on some kind of permanent file. False readings have been reported from steroids, vitamin and herbal concoctions, and prescription medications. There is also a myth that the poppy seeds on hamburger buns can trigger a false reading, but to do that, one would have to consume over five pounds of poppy seeds!

There are always those who try to fool the system, but sooner or later most everyone gets caught. The only real way to pass is to abstain. I used to fill my cup to the rim in rebellion, but realized that it's not the fault of the medical staff. They're just doing their job. I'm sure they don't like taking your urine anymore than you like giving it.

The whole system was a bit silly because the drug test did not screen for alcohol. This meant flight attendants could get in trouble for marijuana they smoked three weeks ago, but someone who drank a bottle of Scotch during the flight would pass. The recent addition of alcohol breathalyzers has sealed the gaps in the drug-testing arena. Now, alcohol tests I agree with, since they test behavior taking place here and now, not two weeks ago. I would say that approximately 40% of flight crews (including myself) are fairly heavy drinkers. Layovers in different cities with different crewmembers bring opportunities for excessive indulgence. If we can't abstain before or during a flight, then we have a serious problem that needs attention.

While there is no way of cheating on the test, there is a way to steer the outcome, although it only works once. If someone gets caught with a positive alcohol or drug test result, it is grounds for dismissal unless they admit that they have a problem. The person declares that they have an addictive personality and a specific addiction. Most companies have detoxification clauses in employment contracts that state the employee must be sent to a rehabilitation center. Once the employee returns to work, the company will then test them on a normal basis. If they fail again, instant dismissal is the consequence. The addictive personality clause is tricky and should only be used as a last resort. A recent incident made me curious if other addictions could be considered in this specific clause.

I was working a night flight to Europe. My First Class passengers were fast asleep, and the sun would be rising soon. I decided to close all of the window shades. In First Class, the seats convert into beds, making it very difficult to reach the windows. Improvising with a coat hanger, I managed to close most of them, but lost my footing while closing the last one and landed in bed with a passenger — unfortunately, a very buxom woman. As I struggled to get to my feet, I grabbed the wrong leverage points. She woke up and started to scream, and all the passengers in the cabin instantly awoke in fear. There I was, messed-up hair, face flushed, standing over an amply endowed screaming woman with two buttons ripped off of her blouse. How was I going to talk my way out of this one?

After profuse apologies, we regained our composure. I asked the woman and another female flight attendant to join me in the galley for a discussion. Luckily, the woman happened to be an airline employee, and after I explained what had happened, she forgave me. She could tell by my demeanor that I was very distraught, and she half-heartedly laughed it off, although I sensed she still had her doubts, for which I didn't blame her in the least.

I wrote up a report just in case it developed into something bigger. What if this lady wasn't as understanding as she seemed to be? She had 12 First Class witnesses to back up her story of a sexual assault. I had a somewhat pathetic excuse and could have gotten into serious trouble. If there had been an investigation into the incident and I was found to have acted improperly, could I have used the addictive personality clause and admitted to a sexual addiction? Or does that work only for politicians and actors?

I am happy to announce that Carol's drug test came up negative. She has since retired and wrote me a letter stating that she is enjoying retirement immensely apart from an occasional flare-up of glaucoma.

The Haunted Skies

Towards the end of the flight you hear a peculiar rustling noise from the overhead bin and a faint ghostly whisper emanating from the back of the airplane. The whisper becomes clearer and spookier.

"Get out!" The whisper gets louder and reminds you of some horror movie. "Get out!" You hear it once again.

No, it's not a ghost but merely the flight attendant waiting for you to disembark so she can go home. But in-flight paranormal activities are common folklore among flight crews. There are the stories of haunted airplanes, airports, and hotels that make their way to the rumor mill from time to time. These are usually the places of bizarre deaths, accidents, or sightings, which I am sure have been exaggerated with time.

While I believe in such occurrences to a minimal degree, I always have found them interesting and a challenge to confront. Growing up, I would have loved to be the one that spent the night in a haunted house or slept at the cemetery. So when a haunted hotel room becomes available, I specifically request that room. Not to be the brave one and impress others, but because I would love to see evidence from the world beyond. Besides a couple of light flickers and a few curtain movements, I had not seen anything convincing me of the afterlife until one winter day.

I was working to Europe with my wife Martha. We had been married for two years and always flew together to maximize our off time since we were busy with schooling and other ventures. During the flight briefing the purser announced the flight details, including the load and aircraft number. A terrified expression appeared on two of the flight attendants' faces.

One of them was normally shy and reserved but she interrupted with, "You know this is the haunted one, don't you?"

"Excuse me?" the purser replied.

"This is the one where eight people died over the Pacific Ocean. The cargo door had ripped off in-flight, sucking several passengers and crew into the engines. The bodies were never located and it is rumored that their spirits haunt the lower galleys."

At that moment the other flight attendant got up, walked out, and put herself on the sick list.

A supervisor appeared and did confirm that this was indeed the refurbished airplane involved in the incident in question, but the haunted rumors were exaggerated and should be disregarded. This, of course, was coming from someone who would not be joining us on the flight. I wasn't worried but rather excited because I was able to hold the senior position of back lower galley and my wife held the forward lower galley. Some of the older 747s had galleys (kitchens) located under the main floor that were accessible by elevators. One of the galleys was located in front for First and Business Class, and the other was in the back for Economy. It was a great position to work, as you are not surrounded by hundreds of people and worked at your own pace. I always carried a mini-stereo and prepped the carts to the beat. The haunted aspect was merely a bonus for Martha and myself.

I have to admit that during my first few minutes in the lower galley I was a little apprehensive, but I shrugged it off and dove right into the service. I listened to the music, prepped the carts, and waited for the meals to finish cooking. Towards the end of the cooking cycle one of the ovens started to turn off and on as if it had a short circuit. Every time an oven shuts off an alarm bell sounds. I gave the oven a brief smack. It seemed to solve the problem for a few minutes until the other ovens joined in. The overhead lights started to dim, and little by little I became concerned. I got a call from my wife in the front galley and she confirmed the same thing was happening with her ovens. With great machismo I blamed it on poor wiring and stated that there was nothing to be worried about. I was trying to convince myself as well.

When the ovens turned off and on, besides the brief alarm bell comes the small whistle of the oven's fans sounding like a ghostly "oooooh" from some bad horror movie. My imagination started to grow and I became slightly nervous. I packed up all the meals and sent them up to the crew to serve. I turned off the ovens, but two of them continued to cycle on and off. The overhead lights went dark and my music started to slow down as if the batteries were old. (Note: I had installed new batteries before the flight.) Now, if you were down below in a small dark room and all of this was happening, I think you would be a bit freaked out as well. I pulled the circuit breaker on the ovens, turned off my music, and surfaced to the main floor to assist in the service. Which, I might add, was not the norm for me.

I wrote up the problem on the airplane's mechanical log and did notice that this specific problem had been written up many times before. The mechanics were unable to rectify the problem, as it only seemed to occur in-flight; when they checked it on the ground the system was fine.

We arrived at the hotel, and the clerk who always likes to save me room #201 (the haunted room) was there with my key set aside from the rest. I kindly requested a different room, having had enough "spirits" for one trip. I realize this type of problem was probably due to poor re-wiring after the accident, but I remain open to other possibilities as well. After that trip I heard about flight attendants bringing Ouija boards or holding séances during crew rests.

Flight attendants have many superstitions, such as not accepting hotel keys with previous air fatality flight numbers, such as: 103, 800, or 911. Did you ever notice that most hotels don't have a 13th floor? Why? Bad luck? Wouldn't this make the 14th floor really the 13th? Many flight attendants won't accept the 14th floor for that very reason.

These superstitions and more are very much alive among many flight crews today. I remember the story about a flight attendant who was extremely superstitious and adamant about following a strict routine of numerology. She would seldom trade her trips, wary about altering fate, and never went against her readings. The beauty of the flight attendant job is its flexibility and the ease of one's schedule. You can work 10 days on and then have 20 days off. You just have to be open to change; she wasn't. On December 18th she got a phone call from a fellow flight attendant about trading a certain trip so she could see her family in New York on the layover. Even though it would benefit the superstitious flight attendant's Christmas schedule, she declined, citing her numbers reading. It was her last flight as that trip was the ill-fated Pan Am Flight #103 that crashed over Lockerbie, Scotland.

Was that her fate? Most probably, but why inconvenience your life worrying about consequences that you have no control over? We are all not long for this world, some more so than others.

Hit Me

A four-hour flight to Las Vegas with a 36-hour layover was too good to be true. Apparently, all of the co-workers who emailed me wanting my trip thought so as well. I hadn't been to Vegas since they opened up the Luxor casino, so I was keeping this trip. A friend had previously joked that I was flying with the "Korean Connection," but I had no clue on what this meant. I didn't think anything of it until the flight.

I walked into the briefing room and was greeted by two Asian men.

"Hey, Frank, I'm Johnny and this is my partner, Nick," a thin Korean man with glasses shook my hand and the other guy waved. Now, when a male flight attendant says partner, they usually mean lover. I didn't have a problem with it, but that was what my friend probably meant by the "Korean Connection."

They were quite fun to work with. It was an easy flight and we all looked forward to a long layover in the exciting city.

"So, what are your layover plans?" Nick inquired.

"I guess I'll do a little gambling and then see the sights," I replied.

"You should hang with us, although you can't tell Nick's wife about the gambling. She is already scared to death that he is on a trip to Vegas with his gambling partner," Johnny teased.

"Ah, I get it; you're gambling partners. I thought that...never mind." I decided to stop there.

"Don't bother with the layover hotel. We have a suite at the MGM waiting for us," Nick said.

"Yeah, right, sure you do," I sarcastically replied.

"Somebody's picking us up from the airport, so we have to change out of our uniforms before we leave the plane."

I shrugged it off but complied and changed in the airplane lavatory on our arrival. We walked out of the airport and headed for a white stretch limousine. The trunk was open, so they started putting their bags in.

"Okay, guys, the gag has gone far enough. You got ..."

The limo driver cut me off. "Hello, Mr. Kim, Mr. Lee. Welcome back. How was your flight?"

"Hey, Jackson, great, thanks. We have a friend joining us this time," Johnny replied.

"Nice to meet you, sir." He opened the door for me and we all drove off.

I was in shock. These guys must have had rich parents, were in the Korean mafia, or were drug dealers. Was that what my friend meant by "Korean Connection"? We didn't make enough money to live like that.

Nick leaned over and whispered in my ear, "By the way, if anyone asks you what you do, you're a dot-commer. Okay?"

I nodded, still confused. We pulled up to the MGM Grand and went up the elevator to the room. The bellhop opened the door to what can only be described as an obscene display of wealth. There were four bedrooms, three bathrooms, and a luxurious living room with a marble Jacuzzi in the center. They tipped the bellhop and he disappeared.

"Okay, what gives? You guys are into illegal stuff, right?"

"No, they just like us here," Nick teased.

I picked up my bag and made a move for the door. "I'm out of here, guys. Thanks for the tour."

"Relax, we're considered VIPs here because of the amount of gambling we do. Haven't you heard of the Korean Connection?" Johnny said reassuringly.

Nick added, "Yeah. All it really means is two Korean guys with a gambling problem. Everything is complimentary — the shows, room service, the drinks, you name it. Now, let's go gamble."

We started off at the $25-minimum black jack table. With my hundred-dollar losing limit, I was out in four hands, but I enjoyed watching Nick and Johnny in action. They moved to the $100-minimum table and were doing pretty well. It was funny when a familiar looking man sat down at our table. He was one of the First Class passengers on the flight. He kept telling us that we looked really familiar but never quite caught on. We just smiled at each other and kept our little secret.

I walked around and watched the gambling as a spectator sport. Throughout the casino most of the eyes appeared dazed and glassy. It's the kind of look I get by the third store when I go shopping with my wife. The Korean Connection's luck started to turn and I had had one too many drinks. I stumbled off to bed while my new friends kept going.

I awoke the next morning to an empty room. I ordered room service, took a shower, and had breakfast out on the balcony. I relaxed by the pool, sipped margaritas, and signed everything to the room. It wasn't every day that I got to live like a king, so I took advantage of every moment. I was getting worried about my Korean friends until I found them at a blackjack table going at it again.

"Hey, guys, what time did you leave the room this morning?" I asked.

"Who left?" Johnny said while Nick yelped at a 21 hand.

"You got to be kidding me."

"No, this is what we do."

They hadn't gotten any sleep but seemed to be in better shape than I was. I left them to it and went to explore the city. Las Vegas is the adult version of Disneyland. If you can get over the cheesy effect that some of the casinos exude, the annoying leaflet distributors, and the long buffet lines, Las Vegas is truly a spectacular experience. I got complimentary tickets to a show and loved it. I had prime rib and red wine back at the hotel and then finished the night off with a cigar and a cognac in the hot tub. The boys were nowhere to be found. I went to sleep wishing them luck and thanking God that I wasn't much of a gambler.

I awoke in the morning to Johnny telling me that we were leaving for the airport in 45 minutes. They were already dressed and having breakfast.

"Did you guys sleep at all?"

"Yeah, we got a couple hours," Nick replied.

"How much did you guys lose?"

"Actually, we're up 11,000 but still down nine, considering we dropped 20 last week," Johnny said as he lit up a cigarette.

"Dollars? You guys are crazy! Anyway, I had a great time at the show. It would have been better with some company."

"You should have asked, the hotel provides that as well," teased Nick.

"That's not what I meant."

We got the limo back to the airport. They tipped Jackson a hundred dollar bill and bade him farewell until next week. They had never been to a show or seen the new additions on the Strip, but the numbers danced furiously in their heads. Somebody hit me if I ever get a gambling problem like that. We changed into our uniforms at the airport, and before long we were on our way back home from a great high-rolling weekend.

Rio Randy

Randy was a shy and mild-mannered flight attendant. He was around my age and we grew to be quite good friends. He mystified us with his obscure author readings and puzzled us with his complex sense of humor. He never seemed interested in the opposite sex or, for that matter, the same sex. He liked to debate even when it was merely for debating purposes. It was the only time I would see him passionate about anything in life.

One day Randy and I had a trip to Rio de Janeiro. A 10-hour flight is a small price to pay for a two-day layover in Rio with a good friend. We met up at the hotel bar after a nap and planned the night's activities. We decided to hit a different club and sample something new. Randy was in an extra-special mood that night and found the smallest things amusing.

We had a couple of Caipirinhas (South American specialty drink) at the new club, and Randy stunned me when he announced his love for a certain girl sitting at the bar. Granted, she was lovely, and this was what happened at such clubs, but this was Randy, never with a girl, usually sexually disinterested, and never on the prowl — Randy.

"Huh, um...go for it, buddy," I mumbled knowing all too well he would never approach her.

"I think I will," he winked at me as he left the table.

Realizing he was about to get severely shut down, I smiled, sipped my drink, and toasted the fact that there might be life in the lower region of his body yet. When he didn't come back right away, I was shocked to discover that he was actually talking with the young lady. I was even more amazed that she seemed fairly interested. He brought her back to our table, where they continued their conversation, with Randy attempting to speak Portuguese. She was lovely, with beautiful hazel eyes and a hypnotic smile. I tried to be somewhat charming, but after a while I could tell they wanted to be alone. I made my excuses, smiled at Randy, and left. You think you know someone but then, girls, another language, and a charmer? "Good for him," I chuckled as I headed back to the hotel.

We had rooms next to each other and as I drifted off to sleep, I heard the unmistakable squeals resound from his room. It was great to hear at first, but soon after I reached for my earplugs. I slept well the rest of the night but couldn't wait to return home to tell all.

I decided not to disturb Randy for morning breakfast, as I was sure room service would be utilized. At pick-up time, I boarded the bus and prepared for the long trip home.

Looking somewhat stressed, a disheveled Randy boarded the bus and approached me.

"Uh, Frank, you got any money?" he sheepishly inquired.

"Just some change and a credit card, why? What's wrong?

"Well, let's say I didn't get exactly lucky last night, just in debt!" he said nervously.

"Oh shit, she was a pro? Did you know?"

"Of course I didn't know! What am I going to do? She won't leave the room until she gets her money."

"Collection time!" It's what we do when a crewmember has a layover monetary problem of some kind.

"No, dude, don't!"

"Ladies and gentlemen, we have a small problem. Randy had a little extracurricular activity last night and, unbeknown to him, it had its price. We need you to give generously to his charity, as we are still a little bit short. He has guaranteed all those who give, details and refunds to be furnished later.

The crew laughed and snickered but gave what they could, which sufficed. He even had enough for a fair-sized tip. He disappeared into the hotel and quickly returned to a standing ovation inside the bus. Randy blushed, but you could just tell he enjoyed the rare occasion of sexual infamy. He was thereafter known around the base as Rio Randy, the stud in South America and a chump among his friends.

I can just see the ads now:

"So, a message to all of you Rio revelers: When cavorting at night down the Brazilian way, bring your cash, because in this land of opportunity she's not going to take IOUs, and she doesn't take American Express!"

Authentic local drink for two – $10
All you can eat beef buffet – $20
The girl you thought you charmed – $75
Newfound ladies' man reputation – Priceless!

Sorry, Randy, but being Frank and all, you just knew I couldn't leave this story out.

Seatbelt Nazi

What is the fascination with the "Seatbelt" sign? Why do so many people ignore it? Is it that people just don't want to be told what they can and cannot do? Maybe people don't realize what they are being protected from. Perhaps the captain forgot to turn the sign off. Maybe the boredom of just sitting there makes people more aware of the urgency building in their bladders. Most flight attendants do sympathize and realize there are times when these nature calls just can't wait.

The seatbelt sign illuminates warning of turbulent weather ahead, the captain makes the announcement, "Seatbelts fastened please," and the flight attendants come around and check, saying the intermittent "Seatbelts, please." Even with the sue-frenzy epidemic in America, it is difficult to believe a judge would award any passenger damages after having been warned three times. I find this sufficient but nevertheless there is always one flight attendant who yells at every passenger disregarding the warnings. Do these flight attendants see it as a rebellion to their job, disrespectful, or a challenge to their authority?

I met a young female flight attendant named Jenny before a flight we were about to work. She had a sweet smile and a shy nature. We were both working in Economy, and her delicate demeanor and pleasant sense of humor indicated she was going to be a real joy to work with.

We prepped the carts after take-off but hit a little turbulence. The seatbelt sign went on, and it was as if a light bulb went off in her head. Jenny's facial expression turned from pleasant to serious in an instant as she stormed up the aisle.

"Seatbelts! You need to fasten your seatbelts!" she said in a loud voice and checked every single seatbelt. As opposed to my muted mumble and occasional glance. Good for her, I thought at first. She was adamant about her checks and took the passengers' safety seriously. After we finished checking, she reverted to her shy demeanor and we continued our conversation.

Then she suddenly looked up the aisle in horror, having spotted a man making his way to the lavatory. She ran to him and lectured him sternly until he obediently returned to his seat. I was a bit mortified at her transformation. It was like Dr. Jekyll and Mr. Hyde playing out in front of me. Slightly comical but unnerving, she continued her tirade every time a passenger got up.

"Don't you know the seatbelt sign is on for a reason? This is for your safety as well as that of the passengers around you! Return to your seat immediately. No, you can't go to the lavatory!"

One passenger managed to slip by her and made it in to the toilet. When Jenny discovered this, she pounded on the door and shouted her lecture between the cracks of the doors. Thinking she might try to unlock the lavatory and open the door, I just stood there with my mouth hanging open in amazement.

"Don't you care about the seatbelt sign?" she shouted at me.

"Uh, yeah, I guess, but if you have to go, you have to go."

"That's just not good enough. We are talking about passenger safety!" She continued to lecture me for the next 30 minutes about the various consequences of turbulence. I tuned out her precise words, but watched her face grow more intense with each point. I suddenly realized that this was the girl who was known throughout the system as the "Seatbelt Nazi." Stories of this type are usually exaggerated, but she more than lived up to her reputation.

Our flight canceled on our return trip so we had the distinct pleasure of dressing in normal clothes and playing passenger for the flight home. I was somewhat relieved I was assigned a seat well away from the seatbelt fanatic. She was nice enough the rest of the time; I just like knowing who I am dealing with all of the time.

I sat next to a flight attendant named Stephanie. She had been on the same flight over but had worked up in First Class.

"So what did you think of Jenny? A bit of a trip?" she asked with a grin.

"Uh, yeah, you could say that. Is she the..."

"The Seatbelt Nazi? That's her. Sure she's a bit mental, but if you had seen what she had, you would be too. What a lot of people don't know is she was the flight attendant taking care of the five-year-old boy who died in-flight on the way to Japan. The child got up to use the bathroom when the seatbelt sign was on, and, the next second, hit the ceiling when the plane hit an air pocket. Rumor has it the little boy died right in her hands."

"Gosh, that explains a lot."

I had renewed respect for Jenny. She had obviously been through a traumatic ordeal that never quite left her. The seatbelt sign came on and I thought of her in a kinder light. I felt guilty at my estranged attitude towards her.

Folks, if the seatbelt sign goes on and you can possibly hold it, wait until the pilots turn it off. It's not worth the risk. The majority of injuries in-flight are caused by turbulence. A close friend of mine recently broke her neck and is currently out on medical leave. Her head hit the airplane's ceiling panel and her neck snapped in two different places. The amount of rehabilitation she needs to go through is frightening. If you think the sign was left on by accident, notify a flight attendant to ask the cockpit. If you can't wait any longer, then do what you've got to do. I feel most of us are adult enough to make these decisions on our own. If you get hurt, the airline probably won't be held liable, but if you hurt anyone else, you can and will be.

I know many of you feel like the flight attendants just enjoy yelling at you and the seatbelt is a perfect excuse, but most of the time they have your safety in mind. I won't yell at you if you disregard the sign, but watch out — Jenny and many other seatbelt soldiers are out there.

Sleeping With the Enemy

After a few years of flying, most flight attendants generally adopt the rule of not dating members of the cockpit. It's not because they are all such a bad bunch, but the few play-boy-cheating-on-the-wife stories that always seem to be prevalent are worth avoiding at all costs. My personal situation is a complete reverse stereotype. My wife is a pilot and I am a flight attendant. I married her when she was a fellow flight attendant and she eventually became a pilot. We are secure in our relationship as I work with many beautiful women and she with many available men. We don't hide our careers from anyone, but you would be surprised how many people hear one statement and process it as another. For example, 50% of our neighbors still believe that she is the flight attendant and I am the pilot.

One day my wife and I went to an elegant, high-level function being thrown for the pilots of her airline. It was

144

not my ideal type of evening but it was important to her. I promised in advance that I would refrain from pilot jokes and be on my best behavior. It was a fancy do and everyone seemed to know my wife. The pilots started in on their technical jargon so I decided to explore the alcohol and appetizer options. The wives gathered on one side of the room and the pilots on the other. The waiters and bartenders were the airline's flight attendants working overtime. I, not knowing anyone, didn't seem to fit into any one group. So I stayed in the quiet and reserved mode while nibbling anything that looked remotely edible.

I listened and observed, thinking of the endless amount of stories that the night would have made. I received many strange looks as if to say, "Who is that, or is he a party crasher?" I knew if I were to approach any one group I would get the standard "We just love your wife, what a wonderful lady she is. What is it that you do?" They would politely smile back when I told them and quickly change the subject. I realized that this was more my "hang-up" as my wife puts it, but usually fairly accurate.

People ask me if I am interested in being a pilot as well. They are always surprised when I respond quickly with an aggressive no. The only interest I have in flying is that my wife loves it and now has a career in the field. She didn't like being a flight attendant, and my firm belief is if you don't like something and you aren't paid well, then you are a fool to continue. My wife is no fool, but I, on the other hand, really enjoy what I do. The diversity of cultures and opportunity to visit places all around the world make my career rewarding. Do I feel awkward serving coffee to a younger female pilot up front, realizing that she is making three times my salary? Sure, a little twinge, but this is only human nature.

After about 45 minutes of increasingly irritated looks from my wife, three drinks, and a copious amount of appetizers, I mustered up enough courage to approach a group of eight pilots by the bar. They seemed like a fun bunch and I was tired of acting the quiet outsider.

"Hey there, how's it going?" I said as all eyes turned to me.

"Hello, we saw you over there, great party, don't you think?" One of them remarked.

"Yes, it is, but do you think an open bar is such a good idea at a pilot function? Everyone is trying to get to-go cups or filling up their flasks." I just couldn't resist and I got a few laughs until they realized I was poking fun at them.

"Do you fly?" one of them asked.

"No, not me."

"Then how are you connected to this function?" Silence hit as the group awaited an answer as if they were suspecting a freeloader on their turf.

"Oh, I am sorry, I'm Frank Steward, Martha's wife..." and in a horrified instant it was time to leave. I walked away from the confused but smirking group and out the front door.

"Wife? What an idiot!" I kept repeating to myself.

Freudian? Maybe. Idiotic? Definitely!

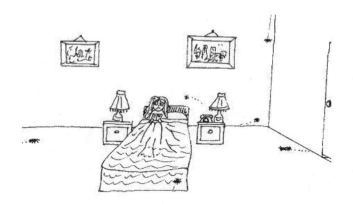

Ladies and Germs

The media has a tendency to scare people into changing their habits. You may think your daily routine is healthy, only to be told that you are doing everything all wrong. One month tap water is bad for you, and the next, bottled water is even worse. Cholesterol this, fat-free that, caffeine bad, coffee good, it's all a bit ridiculous, but it's the media's job to get people to listen; therefore, they bend the truth a bit to suit their stories. My new belief is that red wine is good for you and the media should be taken in moderation.

There are always stories about how unhealthy it is to fly. Among the topics the media has already frightened the public with are the unhealthy cabin air, high fecal count in the airplane's drinking water supply, and the polar radiation involved with longer flights. The story that got many flight attendants buzzing was the one about hotel hygiene.

The media took a special black-light germ finder into the rooms of New York's top ten hotels. Samples were taken for scientific analysis and the results were reported to the public. Among the findings were traces of semen, feces, blood, urine, bugs, and parasites.

Hotels are the flight attendants' second home, so it was no surprise when this story was the sole topic of conversation. It scared many beyond belief. Some flight attendants started bringing their own sheets, pillowcases, towels, and disinfectants. Admittedly, I was concerned, so I purchased one of those black-light pet odor and germ finders. On a layover I performed my own little test. I have to admit I did find a number of suspect stains. I was convinced the media had a valid point, until I turned it on in my own home. My wife and I are quite hygienic, but there were many more areas that lit up in my house than in the hotel room. Okay, we're pet owners, but germs are germs.

We have to face the fact that there are germs everywhere. I found out later from a doctor friend the report didn't tell the public that there were insufficient amounts of any substance found to have any harmful health effects. While it is true I would rather be exposed to germs in my own house than in a hotel, there is a daily maid service in a hotel. When was the last time you disinfected your bathroom? Germs naturally spread. Did you know that germs actually assist and strengthen your body's own immune system?

If you want to be extra careful in hotel rooms, here are a few Frank tips:

1. Wipe down the TV's remote control with an anti-bacterial wipe or a soapy washcloth. Who knows when the

maid last cleaned it or what the previous occupant was doing with it. I found more germs on that little contraption than in the whole room.

2. Rinse out the cups and coffee maker before using them. They are not always cleaned, and, if unused for a while, bacteria can grow.

3. Always fold back the bedspreads and try not to use them. Hotels hardly ever clean them. I found a wide variety of suspicious substances on the two bedspreads I tested.

4. Try to avoid using the telephone in the bathroom. I shudder to think how many people were doing their business while having a chat.

5. Finally, don't be such a hypochondriac; germs are good for you in moderation.

If you are worried, go to the local pet store and pick up a germ/stink finder for twenty bucks. Turn it on in your home first before comparing it to a hotel room. I warn you, though, ignorance is bliss and this might unduly frighten you. If you want to see a light show, turn it on in the airplane's lavatory after a flight. If you are wondering why I am such an advocate of always wearing shoes in there, this is the reason.

Keep the Tip

I initially got interested in the stock market when Albert, a former roommate and flight attendant, read the business section during morning coffee. I had always thought of it as an "old man" thing but the more I heard him talk about it, the more interested I became.

"There it goes again!" Albert yelped.

"What's that?" I asked.

"Pan Am stock price goes to 4 during peak travel season and down to 1 in the slow season. Just like clockwork."

I had never seen anyone get so excited about a stock they didn't own. "Why don't you buy some stock and test your theory?"

"Yeah, with what? You got an extra grand toa lose? Besides, buying stock is just for the bigwigs."

Granted, at that time it wasn't as easy as it is now but there had to be a way to set up an account and test his theory. I put $500 that was supposed to be a car fund into an account and secretly bought 500 shares of Pan Am.

I forgot about it until one day during coffee Albert shook his head and said, "What did I tell you? Pan Am is $4.25 a share!"

I did the math and was amazed that I had secretly made a profit of $2,000. I sold it and then later bought it back at $1. It was brilliant and admittedly not my idea, but who cares? I was on to something. All of a sudden I started joining Albert in the living room for morning coffee and sharing the business section. "Buy this frozen yogurt stock in the winter when it's low and sell it in the summer when it's high. Boeing is basically the only aircraft manufacturer out there and the need for air travel will never cease." It was a no-brainer as he would call it. His ideas were brilliant up until the moment for action. He didn't have the fortitude to take chances on his theories.

Okay, I got stuck in the end with 500 shares of useless Pan Am stock, but I was able to parlay $500 into an amazing $8,500. Barron's newspaper became my bible, and a famous stock picker was my new spiritual leader. I read up on all the latest market activity on every long flight.

One day a man approached me in the back galley and noticed I was reading the business section, " Do you fancy yourself as a bit of a stock picker?"

"Oh, I dabble in the market." I had always wanted to say that.

"Well I have a deal for you. You keep my glass full of that expensive Scotch they have in First Class, and I will give you the biggest tip of your life."

"Sure, why not?" I went up front and got the bottle and filled his glass, feeling skeptical. He told me of a certain

XYZ stock that was going to double in the next six months. I asked him how he could be so sure. He smiled, handed me his card, and walked away. I looked at his card and he was the CEO of XYZ. Was this guy for real?

I told Albert about it, and he scoffed it off as probable BS because it would be insider trading if it was true. I barely knew what a margin call was, much less insider trading. I bit the bullet and bought $5,000 worth of XYZ stock. Only instead of six months it doubled in three. I was in heaven and dreamed of the riches I would attain. When I saw the same man on another flight, I quickly poured expensive Scotch into a glass and delivered it with a smile.

"Hello there, young Frank," he exclaimed. "Did you ever do what I told you to?"

I smiled and handed him the drink. "Thank you."

"If you still have it, then sell it quick. We are headed for a bake sale." He looked around nervously.

A bake sale? That can't be a good thing, so I sold it first chance I got. Two months later an investigation into the books was initiated and the stock lost 85% of its value. It was a lucky escape, but it got me thinking about my choice of working assignments on the plane. I enjoyed the Economy section so much more, but realized the people with all the knowledge were sitting up front.

I overheard conversations between stock analysts and corporation presidents. I would do the research and buy according to what I came up with. I would talk the elite into giving me some kind of information that I could research. Incidentally, I now know what the term "insider trading" means.

Albert soon caught on, and we became a type of long-term day traders. We would buy stocks and sell them within three months. He took up smoking, and we became hooked on video games to pass the time. I was no longer interested in writing, as the game of playing the stock market was addictive and much more lucrative. At the peak, my trading account was up to 200K and looking back was not an option. All went well until March of 2000 when, even though we saw it coming, the bottom dropped out of the bag. The stock market tumbled, as did the number of zeros in my portfolio. My so-called famous stock guru always said to remain long term and never jump out. Well, his face is now on my dartboard and my account is no longer smiling. Hence, you are reading this book.

So, as the saying goes, I didn't quit my day job. It was fun while it lasted and I can say I learned a lot. I still listen and take notes when people talk stocks up front, but I now do it more with an air of skepticism.

A few Frank pieces of stock advice:

1. There is no such thing as a sure thing.

2. Do extensive research. More often than not, people who offer a stock tip are only trying to boost their company.

3. If you get out when your stock doubles and then the stock subsequently triples, be happy, because a gain is a gain.

4. Invest only what you can afford to lose. The dollars may dance furiously in your head, but losing your life savings and emergency reserve is hard to deal with.

5. Don't put all of your eggs in one basket. Don't have your investments tied up in the same company you are depending on for a pension. It is a point that has recently caused much grief in the business world and especially the airline industry.

They have a saying in England, "Bob's your uncle." Loosely, it means that everything is as it should be and all events happen for a reason. Well, Bob really is my uncle, and in the peak of my stock-picking days I discovered that he, too, was a big stock enthusiast. We had stock competitions and exchanged ideas. He gave me sound advice, and I replied with long shots promising big payouts. He bought the "older man" stocks and I bought the wild roller coaster stocks. I now know why they are called "older man" stocks, because their owners know better. Wisdom comes with age and experience; I now own the "older man" stocks and just hope he didn't follow any of my tips. Regardless, "Bob's still my uncle."

The Italian Sweater

When I first started working as a flight attendant, all of the people with whom I went through training were too junior to hold good destination trips. Either they were stuck on reserve (on call) or were assigned the trips that nobody wanted. I was German-language qualified, so I got great trips but flew with mainly older flight attendants. They were very nice to work with, but let's just say "painting the town red" on a layover was something I had to do alone.

One December, many years ago, I had a whole month of Berlin trips. As it was an especially cold winter day, I thought I would stay in the hotel for the duration of the layover. Christmas was approaching and I wanted to rest up for the holiday season. I had heard our hotel was supposed to have the best sauna in Europe, so I decided to check it out.

While on layovers I didn't like standing out as a tourist, so I always tried to blend in as much as possible. In the locker room, I noticed the men walking in from the sauna were naked. I figured there were separate saunas for men and women, so I followed suit, or I should say, suit-less. The sauna consisted of seven different sections, each having specific directions for use. For maximum results, the user should enter each section for 10 minutes and then move to the next. I was given a timer that would go off every 10 minutes.

I walked into the first station, which was a eucalyptus steam room, designed to open the pores. I removed my towel and reveled in the heat. There is something decadent about soaking in a sauna when you know it's snowing outside. A few minutes later, the door opened and five gorgeous Alitalia Airline flight attendants walked inside. I knew they worked for Alitalia because I had seen them in the hotel lobby when I checked in. My first thought was that I was in the women's sauna and they were about to scream. Stretched out, butt naked and fearing their reaction, I quickly closed my legs.

To my surprise they hardly took notice of me and removed their towels. So there I was, 22 years old, naked in a sauna with five equally naked Italian women, praying with all my might that an embarrassing body reaction was not a certainty. I had lived in Germany for a few years before the airline job, and learned, somewhat, to deprogram the taboo about public nudity that was so prevalent in America. But I was a young man at my sexual peak and this was going to be hard (no pun intended).

I started to relax as my fears began to fade. I felt wonderful, not in a sexual way, but in a peaceful way. I was in a room of naked people, without issues or uneasy feelings. It felt totally natural. Then my timer went off and everyone turned and stared at me. I got up and moved on to the second room. It was an extremely hot sauna with the smell of lavender. I relaxed, and sure enough three minutes later my five young ladies joined me. Each one was beautiful in her own right, with a different shape and distinctive characteristics.

The pattern of changing rooms continued for the next three stations. We didn't bother putting our towels back on between rooms, and I even managed to carry on a short conversation with a couple of them. There were no incidents of blood rushing to the wrong part of my body as previously feared. Maybe I was just growing up.

I got to the sixth section, which consisted of stairs leading up to a small plunge pool. According to the directions, I was to immerse myself in the cold water and jump up and down, splashing water over my body. I was proud of my newfound maturity, but cold water and naked man were not a good mix. I skipped the sixth station and headed for number seven.

This section was a sauna with a glass front looking out on the plunge pool. One by one, my lovely Italian women took their turns jumping in while bathing and splashing. There I was, facing out with nowhere else to look. It was as if I had front seat tickets at a show. I guess I could have closed my eyes but of course didn't consider that possibility. Who designed this layout? By the time the fourth plunge pool contestant jumped in, my age took over and no amount of depressing thoughts could make the reaction subside. I wrapped the towel around me in a convenient pinning manner and made my escape.

It was a great sauna but was it "therapeutic"? I had difficulty sleeping or concentrating throughout the layover. The naked body is a wondrous and beautiful creation. Everyone is undoubtedly self-conscious about one thing or another but you should never be embarrassed of it. If you get an opportunity to take a similar sauna, give it a try. So what if you have a little extra weight or your dimensions aren't up to par with those of other people. Celebrate the differences and shed your hang-ups. You will probably find the experience soul gratifying and quite liberating. With all of this said, I still recommend that men should trust me and stay away from cold water.

While in Europe, you may want to ask about specific sauna dress codes because surprises come in different shapes and sizes. Never assume anything.

Stars in the Skies

I have always felt a bit sorry for traveling celebrities. Even though they are usually in a higher class of service on the plane, all eyes, cameras, and conversations are riveted on them. Autograph-seekers, members of the media, and the curious pass by their seat in hope of a glimpse. Gawkers may try to act discreet, but the celebrities know exactly what they're doing. While it is all part of the price of fame, the constant eye of scrutiny is undoubtedly difficult to cope with.

Some of the celebrity in-flight hardships that I have witnessed include ripped clothing, soap opera villains spat on, personal items stolen, drunken advances, panty delivery, and even a mauling by a star-struck fan. There is even a flight attendant that I fly with who works for a well known tabloid. He secretly takes pictures and reports on celebrity behavior in-flight.

I have served many stars in my flying career but try to treat them as ordinary passengers. Many celebrities whom I expected to be a problem turned out to be quite pleasant. Conversely, I have been appalled by the rudeness of a few whom I had expected to have pleasant personalities based on their public persona. You can never tell with actors what they will be like in the flesh. This is mainly because when you see them as the villain or hero in a movie, they are only acting. Quite often, they turn out to be the opposite of their movie or television characters. For example, Carroll O'Connor, who played the grumpy Archie Bunker, was the nicest celebrity I have ever met.

The runner-up for Frank's best celebrity in-flight passenger goes to Roger Moore. Yes, James Bond himself was sitting in my First Class section on a flight from London. After takeoff, I quickly went to his seat to take his drink order, eager to ask the question, "Shaken or stirred?"

"Miller Lite please." My excited smile faded, as he continued in his proper English accent, "You don't know how many people I disappoint with that reply. I actually detest martinis." He was very polite and had many stories to tell. The winner of my favorite celebrity "award" goes to Lesley Nielsen, from such movies as Airplane, The Naked Gun, and Police Squad. He was sitting in First Class on his way to film a commercial in London. We were delayed on the ground for about two hours, but he didn't mind. He was polite, cheerful, and friendly. Once we took off, he began studying his commercial script. It was my first time as purser, so for most of the flight I was running around making sure that everything was going smoothly.

When the first film was over, I looked through the selections and found his movie, The Naked Gun. It wasn't scheduled, but I put it in to see if I could get a reaction from our star up front. He didn't notice for the first half hour, as he was busy reading. I began to worry that he might not appreciate the joke or the attention it could bring. He finally glanced up at the screen, did a double take, and started to chuckle. He turned to me, pointed his finger, and got out of his seat.

"Very good. Now watch this," he said, as he walked down the aisle. Pausing at every screen in the Business and Economy cabins, he watched intently, making a funny expression until people noticed who he was. Every cabin had a good laugh and gave a round of applause. He then returned to his seat and picked up his script.

Honorable mention goes to the actress famous for the voice of Bart Simpson. She was invited up into the cockpit and made the captain's announcements, which had everyone in hysterics.

I had a lifelong crush on a certain actress until she succeeded in making a 10-hour flight unbearable for everyone. She had made her start in horror films and was the girl who always got away from the bad guy in the end. On the flight she complained about everything, drank too much, and acted like a passenger from hell. Now, every time I see an old movie of hers, I root for the bad guy.

A certain male tennis star wins the prize for the rudest celebrity. He injured a gate agent, yelled non-stop at the crew, and ruined everyone's flight. Someone needs to tell him to grow up, and I am being serious!

A certain female talk show host demonstrated very conspicuously that she disliked all flight attendants. She always had her assistant with her, who would do all the talking for her. We weren't permitted to talk directly to her. The assistant repeated everything to the celebrity as if she didn't hear the flight attendant. She came across as snobbish, spoiled, and having an extreme holier-than-thou attitude-the complete opposite of her demeanor in her professional life. What she didn't realize was that flight attendants can be the source of the best or worst publicity you could ever imagine. They talk to other flight attendants, passengers, and anyone else who will listen to their stories. One bad move by a celebrity can go a long way.

When I first started flying, we had a passenger who was a young comedian just starting out in show biz. He was sitting in Economy, but his seat was broken, so he hung out in the galley and chatted with the crew. I remember one thing he said quite clearly: "Somebody should write a book about the characters and incidents in the airline industry. All of this would be great material." That man was Jay Leno, current host of The Tonight Show.

If you notice a celebrity in-flight and wish to get an autograph or to meet them, avoid approaching them directly. They may be having a bad day or not want the attention. Contact a flight attendant first to ask the person if it would be all right to approach them. Celebrities usually are courteous and amenable to requests, unless, of course, they have their assistants with them.

Going Dutch

Jack was a fairly shy and new pilot for our airline, and right out of the military. Except for a rare military flight, he had never been out of the country. At our pre-flight briefing, everyone could tell by his wide-eyed grin that he was looking forward to our international trip.

"It's my first time to Amsterdam, and I am bringing along my digital video camera to capture the trip. My buddies in the military will get a kick out of it," Jack said, like a schoolboy getting ready for "Show and Tell."

"You know you won't be allowed to film in the Red Light District?" I replied, getting a few laughs.

"Why not?" Jack asked, seemingly discouraged.

"The prostitutes are very picky about that sort of thing. They smash cameras on the ground if they catch you, or so I am told." A few more laughs and the briefing was over.

The flight was fairly uneventful, and Jack made his rounds while filming everything from the airplane's interior to the view from 35,000 feet. We got to the hotel, and the crew agreed to meet up after a nap to see the sights of Amsterdam.

We went to the museums, Anne Frank's House, and then on to the Heineken Brewery for a tour. No visit to Amsterdam is complete without a stroll down the Red Light District. It's fun, interesting, and quite harmless. The ladies of the night were in their windows and the smell of marijuana smoke lingered in the air.

Jack tried to film a bit, but was told almost immediately by a local to put the camera away or lose it. He was extremely disappointed because that was what he wanted to film the most. I told him he could always film the racy after-hour television programs when he got back to the hotel. As a consolation prize, we went to the sex museum, had a few drinks, and marveled at the people smoking pot out in the open. We were floored when a couple of the girls on the crew suggested we see a sex show. They had always wanted to but never had the courage. There was confidence in numbers, so we all went and had a good laugh, too. The show was well done, and while I would recommend it only for people with open minds, I also suggest staying out of the first couple of rows — trust me on this.

We boarded the plane the next day, laughing and talking about a great layover. Unfortunately, we were informed of a three-hour flight delay, so they held off passenger boarding. We all made ourselves comfortable in a First Class seat and decided to watch a movie.

On his way to do the customary airplane walk-around inspection, Jack asked, "Do you want to see my layover video?" A resounding yes was returned from a now bored crew. "But you have to be aware that I did film some of an uncensored television movie last night."

"Oh, please, we went to a sex show together, you can drop the PC crap," one of the women remarked.

So Jack popped in the videotape, pushed "Play," and walked off the plane to perform his inspection. We all sat around watching and laughing at the video. Near the end, Jack had placed the camera on a bedside table and filmed a Dutch pornographic movie. After a few minutes everyone started feeling a bit uncomfortable. It wasn't like the previous night, where we all had a few drinks and were caught up in the moment.

One of the female flight attendants sat up and pointed at the screen. "What is that?"

"If you don't know, I can't tell you," I wisecracked.

"No, not that — that, on the side." She walked to the screen and pointed at a faint reflection.

The more we looked, the clearer the image became. The reflection was of Jack, and, let's just say, he was reacting to the movie with his hands full. We were shocked at first, and then came a chuckle or two, progressing to outright hilarity. There wasn't a dry eye among the crew. The other two pilots came to witness the laughter, and joined in as well. Just as Jack's reflection was "finishing up," so to speak, Jack returned from his walk-around. "What's so funny?"

The crew erupted in roaring laughter. I laughed so hard I think I pulled a groin muscle. Jack's confused expression merely added fuel to the fire. It took a good 15 minutes for anyone to be able to explain the hilarity to him. When someone finally did, he was unable to look at anyone directly in the eye for the remainder of the flight. He had a permanent blush and never emerged from the cockpit. I think each one of us laughed our way across the Atlantic — all of us, that is, except Jack.

Jack was on his first foreign trip, brand-new pilot with our airline, but became instantly known around the system as "First Officer Whacker." It's a name that follows him to this day, but he was recently promoted to "Captain Whacker."

Flight crews never forget, and I am sure he will take the name into his retirement years. We could give him a break, but never seem to let Captain Jack off — the hook, that is.

Life's Hurdles

I hate envy. It's an addictive emotion that is fed to us by people with low self-esteem and stoked by the media. An actor makes countless millions for each movie, or some athlete signs a multi-million-dollar sports deal. So and so is beautiful and thin and J. Grisham hits the bestseller list yet again. I try to stay away from all of it but I can't seem to escape entirely. I envy my cat! He lives the life that I would die for. He sleeps 18 hours a day, eats, carouses at night, and then sleeps some more. He doesn't have a care in the world, likes a good rub occasionally, and is pretty much able to amuse himself when needed.

Before a flight, I always run around the house securing this, cleaning that, and generally prepping for a few days away from home. My cat stares at me from his favorite spot as if I am a madman. It's as if he is telling me to relax and not to take life so seriously. I try to emulate my feline's philosophy (is this where we get the term "copy-cat"?) but I usually revert back to the typical stressed Virgo personality.

It seems everything in life is an obstacle. *"As soon as I get out of school . . ." "After I get my promotion . . ." "When the kids move out . . ."* It's not until we grow old that we realize those obstacles weren't obstacles at all; they were life, with the final obstacle being death. My grandmother always used to say, "Nobody is truly happy until they die." She lived until the age of 92.

No obstacles have been more apparent to me than my wife's never-ending struggle to become a pilot. She came home one day after working a flight as a flight attendant and announced, "I am going to be a pilot."

I thought she was having an early mid-life crisis. We were running a catering business and had seriously discussed having children. Martha's grandfather was a WWII pilot, and as a young girl in England, she expressed an interest in becoming a pilot when she grew up. She was told that women became stewardesses and men flew the airplanes. After joining the airline as a flight attendant, she soon discovered that this was not the case. She had never flown a plane before but was positive that she wanted to be a pilot.

"Okay, dear, you be a pilot," I said sarcastically, knowing very well it would never become a reality.

Lo and behold, she did just that and now is a pilot for a commuter airline — an achievement that was not without hard work, considerable expense, and determination. The hurdles along the way were many. At maximum stress capacity, she would always come to me before a major test or license check ride and state that if she only passes this one obstacle, then she will be happy. She passed every time and was happy for about one hour, and then it was on to the next stage. The obstacle list was endless: private pilot license, instrument, commercial, ratings such as: CFI, CFII, MEI, then on to the airline interview process: the hiring, the wait in the pilot pool for training, ground school, flight school, probation, upgrade to jet, upgrade to captain, and finally on to the major airlines to do it all over again.

"Just one more hurdle and I will finally be happy," she would tell me over and over again.

The point that she isn't getting is that all of these obstacles aren't the burdens of the job; they are the job.

Just as it is in life, you won't be happy suddenly when you get to that much sought after marker — different job, kids graduate, retirement, etc. You have to be happy now and embrace the obstacles as challenges and a part of living.

But then again, I'd still rather be my cat.

Terminal 5

Frankly Venting

Pass the Buck

You get to the airport and see the laborious lines at the check-in counter. This is because of spring break travel, the agent informs you. Then you head to the security section, the slow moving lines, near cavity searches and confusion- -this is due to the 9/11 tragedy. You get to your gate and your flight is delayed — due to weather. After boarding the aircraft, you realize your aisle exit row seat is actually an extra-small seat in the middle. The boarding agent blames an aircraft configuration change. In flight you don't get your special meal, and the flight attendant tells you that catering hasn't been up to par lately. Your video screen isn't working for the movie, and your seat partner informs you it's because of the mechanic slow-down the airline's having.

You land late and miss your connecting flight — as the customer service agent tells you it is the fault of your travel agent, who did not leave enough time in between flights.

Just once, would it kill one person to apologize and take responsibility for the situation? No, that's not going to happen, since this game is called "Pass the Buck." There are no winners in this game that all airlines seem to play well. When I flew for a different airline, I used to apologize at least a hundred times a flight. I once thought the airline's motto should have been "We're Sorry." I didn't realize that what I was doing was weighing myself down. After a while, the apology, whether you mean it or not, can have a lasting psychological affect. So now, I am sorry to say, I play the game.

Any big airline consists of many departments — ground staff, pilots, flight attendants, and mechanics, to name a few. Each department is responsible for a different facet of the passengers' traveling experience. If one facet breaks down, it usually has a ripple effect on the other parts. Eventually, this permanently influences your mind-set and sours your opinion of air travel. Take the On Time Arrival aspect. On the surveys that some passengers actually fill out, the On Time Arrival is considered one of the most important aspects by far. So in an attempt to boost those statistics and ultimately win your business, airline management has made it the top priority. Screw service, self-respect, and, incredibly enough, sometimes safety; if we get you there on time, we have done our job.

If a flight leaves or arrives late, management wants to know whom to blame. Every time they pin the blame on one department, it's called "taking the delay." Too many of these blames and "heads will roll." So, now, all too often, you will see someone from one employee group arguing with another.

"Flight attendants are going to take the delay on this one," a gate agent spouts.

"It's not our fault there is a mechanic on board. We're not taking the delay," the flight attendant replies.

"You called us for this problem, you should take it," the mechanic points at the gate agent.

At that moment a pilot walks down the jet way, obviously late for the flight. All three smile at one another as they now have their blamee.

Oh, for goodness sake! It's like little kids fighting in the sandbox. It's very unprofessional, but as long as they have their scapegoat, Daddy's not going to yell at them.

Ultimately, this whole fiasco is your fault because you chose that airline in the first place. Let the games begin.... and please believe me when I say that I am sorry but this is because the bigger the airline, the more people to blame.

Did you see how I conveniently passed the buck just then?

What a Waste

We are fortunate enough to live in a time of plenty where starvation in this country is rare. Our food production is at such levels that wastage is a normal occurrence, and two-thirds of all Americans are deemed overweight. Our government subsidizes farmers to produce surpluses that often are just left to rot, and the cycle of waste continues from store to consumer.

The wastage in the airline industry is no different. The amount of trash and wasted food that accumulates is staggering. Yes, believe it or not, even though it seems like they're not feeding you much, they waste as much as they use. The amount of recycling that should take place but doesn't is mind-boggling. Now, I hate those people who complain but offer no solution, so I have one. The government should crack down on wasters and reward recyclers in the form of tax incentives. Corporations these days claim recycling costs too much, but if this is the case, then something should be done to make it uneconomical not to conserve.

The airlines should initiate programs that will encourage employees not to open items until necessary, reuse and take steps toward recycling. I know most flight attendants would be more than happy to conserve, for the landfills are filling, and tomorrow's children will inherit today's mess and lack of vision.

Alice was a flight attendant who was always passionate about the wastage and non-recycling issues of the world and her airline. She was in her mid-fifties and around 40 pounds overweight. She was on a layover with her friends when one of them challenged her to do something about her passion. It was then the dare took shape. She had always claimed that she could easily live off of what the airlines waste each flight. By the end of the evening the group had hammered out the following rules:

1. For one entire year, Alice could not purchase or consume any food that was not from one of her flights. This included off-time and vacation as well. The only exception was the fruit or vegetables she grew in her garden.

2. Cat food was the only food allowed for purchase, so her cats would perhaps eat better than Alice — or at least more consistently.

3. Alcohol was considered the same as food and was to be put into a flask at the end of a flight, instead of pouring it down the drain.

4. She was allowed one meal at a restaurant per month, but only if she didn't pay for the bill.

5. Each friend would pay $500 if Alice made it, and she in turn agreed to pay each friend $250 if she didn't.

Alice thought this would be a great way to save money, lose weight, and make a valid point. She called it her personal In-Flight Survivor. It was a bit risky as such tactics are considered pilfering by the company, and most international customs authorities frown at any food items in your bags.

She took the fruit left on the unused breakfast trays, cereals, yogurts, bread rolls, and made sandwiches from the leftover deli platters. She had the most impressive sized flask and was a walking ad for Tupperware. I met Alice halfway through her challenge, and by that time she was known as the Tupperware lady. She carried every type of container possible. She admitted that it was tough during vacations, but she had her stock of frozen items and was well prepared. Unfortunately, it was hard for her to get a second date, as she would gorge herself silly at each month's outing.

After the first month, it became a lifestyle for Alice. She once flew to Paris First Class, and got on a return flight home the very same day. This way she was treated to two First Class meals and didn't break the deal. She was determined to make it, and looked upon the dare as an adventure in an alternative lifestyle.

She called me the day after winning the challenge. Her friends had thrown her a party and presented her with winnings of $4,000. She had lost 40 pounds, estimated her grocery bill savings at $9,000, and was planning to run a marathon in a couple of months. Okay, her cholesterol and blood pressure were a great deal higher than normal, but you can't have everything.

Modern technology is great, but it is encouraging physical laziness in people. From remote controls to wireless functions, bottom line...lazy. Modern conveniences should take into account conservation as well. I was sure this was not the case until I experienced a lengthy airport delay between flights. I walked around the new high-tech airport and examined technology at its finest. From the moving walkways to Internet kiosks, I looked for the conservation aspects.

The doors opened automatically as I walked into the restroom. The urinal had a sensor and flushed for me. When I washed my hands, the water turned on and off by itself, as did the hand dryer. What I didn't realize at first was, besides the lack of germ transmission and ease, was the monumental amount of water and electricity it saved. Previously, faucets that were left on or paper wasted cost society millions. The closer I looked around me, the more evidence I found of cost savings in modern technology.

I left the airport restroom through the automatic doors, not touching anything the entire process — well, almost nothing. But if modern technology ever gets to the level of the automatic zipper-upper or the bottom-wiper, that's where I draw the line!

Can't Handle the Truth

These days, passengers have demanded and won the right to know the truth behind a flight's mechanical problem. This right is in the new "Passenger Bill of Rights." Maybe you can handle the truth, but I know from previous experience I can't always stand to hear it. It's like if all politicians had to tell the truth, would you really want to hear it?

Ignorance is bliss in most of the situations dealing with mechanical delays. Most of the time, the cockpit doesn't know what's wrong, only that they can or cannot go. If all pilots told you the exact truth and held nothing back, it would sound something like this:

> "Ladies and gentlemen, this is Bob from the cockpit. God, I love the way I sound over this Passenger Address system. Anyway, we have a little blinking light that's not supposed to be blinking. We have tapped it a couple times and it still seems to be blinking.

So we are going back to the gate to get a blinking light specialist to put a sticker on it stating that it's okay to blink. None of you will make your connections, but we appreciate you flying "Honest Airlines."

"Our lead mechanic is on his lunch break and won't be back for two hours. Since we need his signature and the mechanics are currently in contract negotiations, we will not be going anywhere for another one hour and 59 minutes."

"Ladies and gentlemen, this is generally a crappy airline and today is no different from the rest..."

"We don't know what's wrong, but for some reason the airplane is not starting."

"Every time we push the throttle forward, fuel gushes out of the left engine. This can't be good, so we are having someone check it out."

"Management didn't plan right this month, as we don't have anyone scheduled to fly you to your destination."

"We are canceling this flight because we need this airplane to fly to a more lucrative destination with more booked passengers."

"The whatchamacallit won't fit into the doo-hickey, so we have to have a new doo-hickey flown in from Missoula, Montana, but the next flight doesn't leave from there until tomorrow night."

Too much information is not always a good thing. The truth can be off-putting and many times not too reassuring. I agree it is important to tell it like it is about the time expected and the general nature of the problem, but I also feel that the specifics can, and probably should, be avoided. I got inspired to write this chapter after a Captain, adhering to the Passenger Bill of Rights, disclosed the information that made everyone, including myself, feel very uneasy. The only thing he was able to accomplish was to generate a consensus of doubt about his flying competency.

Next time you experience a mechanical delay, ask yourself one question: Do you really want to hear the truth?

First Class Baby

Picture this: You scrimp and save because you swore the last time you flew Economy, it would be the last time. You've come to the conclusion that you are fed up with the small seats, meager meals, and wine with screw-off tops. It is time for a little class in your life. It took you a couple of months to rationalize the First Class fare is three times that of the Economy fare, but your sanity is worth it.

You make your way to the First Class lounge, grab a paper and have a steaming hot cup of coffee until the boarding of your flight is announced. You get to your seat on the plane; someone hangs up your jacket and offers you a pre-departure cocktail. Now this is living, you think to yourself, realizing you have made the right choice in ticket selection. The door is ready to close when you see a mother and a crying infant step onto the airplane. You glance at the empty seat next to you and in an instant, fear for the worst. You pray, hope and fantasize this lady passes you and heads for Economy. Instead, she plops her baby onto the seat, stows her bag in the overhead bin, and hands a baby bottle to the nearest flight attendant.

No, this couldn't be. It's not supposed to happen this way, you think to yourself as the infant glares at you in between screams. The baby is secretly telling you that he is going to make your flight hell. You quickly put your headphones on over your earplugs and try to block out any sign of the neighbor seat. After take-off, the little rascal vomits on your shoes and you can just tell that the other end of him has produced a similar aromatic present. You can't complain to the flight attendant because it would make you seem like the most evil of passengers. Quite frankly, what could the flight attendant possibly do? Nothing. And this is exactly what they will tell you.

"You were a child once, too, you know?" is a possible snippety mother's reply.

"Yes, but I never flew First Class."

The kicker of the whole story is that the lady with the infant is oftentimes an employee or upgrade. So she isn't even paying for her ticket!

Now, this angers me to no end. In my opinion, children under a certain age should not be allowed to sit in First Class, no matter if they are paying for it or not. It's not fair. The baby doesn't appreciate the complex service. There is probably a seat in the back with a spare next to it so the baby can move around, and everyone else in the First Class cabin can enjoy their journey that much more. No offense to those of you in the Economy section, but from time to time a baby or two is expected back there.

I have been in many debates about this with mothers, fellow workers, and passengers. I believe it should be a First Class law. Some airlines already have those regulations, but not any American carriers that I know of. Maybe they are fearful of offending somebody. Well, by not enforcing rules such as these, they are offending everyone else in the cabin. Airlines need those passengers willing to pay a higher price, but are usually oblivious to their common gripes. Business people and upscale travelers, I urge you to write to your airlines and demand it. They will eventually listen to you if you threaten your loyalty.

Meanwhile, realizing the baby is not going to stop yelling, you get up, walk to the back, and search for an empty seat away from the screaming little bundle of goo. Your First Class fantasy, and all the money it involved, has just been trashed right down the diaper shoot.

C'est La Vie.

Air's Discouraging Words

As the song goes "where seldom is heard, a discouraging word, and the skies are not cloudy all day." Unfortunately, in the airline business this is not the usual case. Many poorly chosen words are uttered by passengers to flight attendants, and while we have become accustomed to hearing them, they are never easy to digest.

The following is Frank's top ten list of most discouraging overheard remarks.

1. "You look tired." I never understood this saying's intent. It is a no-win statement. If the flight attendant wasn't tired, you have just made her feel it, and if she is truly tired you have now made her feel doubly so.

2. During boarding a frustrated passenger announces to the flight attendant, "I am never flying this airline again." Now my question is, why would anybody say that, especially at the beginning of a flight? At that moment we are probably thinking, "good riddance" plus if you aren't going to fly on our airline again, we don't really care if you have a good flight or not, and will therefore probably not treat you so royally.

3. Our airline threatens to go into bankruptcy protection and instead of common courtesy or concern for our careers, the passengers ask about the status of their frequent flyer points should the airline go under. While we realize that it is a genuine concern for them, a little consideration for the future of airline employees would be appreciated. What's even worse is that our friends and families usually ask this as well.

4. While boarding, a passenger comes up to me and whispers in my ear, "I have a bad feeling about this flight." They haven't seen anything or heard specific threats, but they have a "bad feeling." If you have a bad feeling about a flight, don't spread your doubts to me. I can't go to the captain with, "I think we better cancel because the lady in 21A has a bad feeling about the flight." If I am superstitious, then I will be on edge the entire trip.

5. "Smile!" Sounds like a fairly harmless saying, but it is another of those no-win statements. If the flight attendant is truly in a bad mood then she will be even more so upon hearing this. If she isn't in a bad mood, you have just placed her in one. I fly with an elderly lady who always looks like she is frowning, even when she is actually smiling. She got so fed up with people telling her to

smile that she now tells them that her husband died yesterday. It makes the person who said it feel incredibly guilty and simultaneously teaches them a lesson. I took a survey of 50 flight attendants and while most of them would just let the comment pass, all of them reacted negatively, with 37 telling me that they would be thinking — and I quote — "up yours!"

6. A passenger in Economy was flirting with an elderly flight attendant, who was somewhat interested until the fatal line of "You must have been a knock-out." Her smile promptly turned into a scowl and the possibility of a future date was gone. The words "must have been" should stay well away from any pick-up line. Believe it or not, I have heard it said several times, and not once did it go over well. Incidentally, this also qualifies as the worst inflight pick-up line next to remarks about the "mile-high club applications."

7. "I wouldn't want your job for anything!" At that point, probably neither do we.

8. "Eew, what are you eating?" If the meal I was enjoying doesn't look appealing to you, don't say anything. Better yet, don't watch me eat.

9. "When is the baby due?" Three, two, one, kaboom! "I'm not pregnant!" Oops. Now, with the absence of the weight policy, this happens more than you think. On that same subject, "Why don't you have children?" Oh, a common but big mistake. Before you ask that, have you considered the possibility that he or she may not be physically able to and this fact is breaking her heart?

10. "These in-flight meals are horrible!" Whether it is the quality or quantity, I have no say in the matter. The only aspect of the meal I am responsible for is the temperature of the entree. If it's too cold or burnt, then it's my fault. Funny thing is now that many of the flights are non-catered, the same people who complained before, are now complaining of hunger. Be careful of what you wish for, it might just come true. What's worse than being forced to eat airplane food? Having to pay extra for it.

Bible Bob

The variety of the flight attendants I fly with is quite diverse. When I meet someone for the first time, I like to listen and grasp their views and perceptions of the world. I believe that everyone has something to offer, good and bad. Very rarely do I pass judgment or frown on the beliefs of others, although, when my wife once returned home in tears due to another flight attendant's views, I was quick to defend. Apparently, she had flown with the infamous "Bible Bob," a male flight attendant who used religion and the Bible as his weapon. His aggressive bullying tactics would have most co-workers furious and many fearful after working with him. Rarely would a report be filed against him, as religious persecution is a tough case to pursue. I had heard of this character before through the grapevine, but had not yet flown with him. I didn't even know his real name, as Bible Bob was just a nickname.

My wife is a strong-willed individual, but after four days of constant hell berating, she let him get to her. As she explained what had happened, she placed some religious literature on the kitchen table in front of me — titles such as *Why You Are Going to Hell*, *How to Make It to God*, and *Sinners Repent*. His ability to steal energy from people and feed his own inner being was nothing short of evil. My wife mistook that evil for her newfound feelings of guilt.

I was furious. I wanted to give Bob a piece of my mind. Nobody has the right to force his or her religious beliefs on anyone, much less cast dispersions. Religion is supposed to be beautiful, not hurtful. It took a while for me to console Martha and in turn for her to calm me down. I agreed not to actively pursue a showdown, but secretly longed for the day when we would fly together.

About a year later in a pre-flight crew briefing, I spotted a male flight attendant holding a Bible instead of the in-flight manual as normally required. "It couldn't be," I thought at first.

The man leaned over to another crewmember and said, "This is the only manual I will ever need."

With that comment I was certain he was Bible Bob. Intense anger and excitement grew inside me. I decided to back off at first, because such emotions were not normal for me. I played it cool in-flight and wouldn't talk to him unless he came to me first. The majority of the flight he was preaching to a newly divorced flight attendant who, I could tell by her expressions, was not the better for his lecture. He twisted beautiful, majestic biblical phrases into a bitter and hateful sermon, leaving sorrow and guilt in his wake. I watched him as he even took a pair of scissors to the in-flight magazines, cutting out what he called "the devil's text."

Towards the end of the flight he approached me in the galley. "Frank, what's your story?"

"What do you mean?" I played naïve as the other crewmembers pretended not to listen.

"Are you going to heaven or hell?" he sneered.

I took a deep breath and then let loose. "Listen here, I've heard of you and your God-fearing antics. My wife came home in tears because of you. You unload all of your insecurities on people, steal their energy, and call it God's work. You are pure evil and should mind your own business when it comes to religion. You're the reason people turn away from, instead of embrace, God! That...is my story!"

Everyone in the galley, including Bob, was stunned. It took a second for him to regroup and then he responded loudly, "You know you're going to hell, don't you?"

"Well, I guess I will see you there then!" I got up and walked down the aisle with my head held high. We didn't speak afterwards, but all of the other flight attendants thanked me profusely.

Bible Bob is no longer flying as a flight attendant. Rumor has it he got into a heated discussion with an equally passionate male Jewish flight attendant and apparently fists were thrown. That and the fact that our company began allowing travel benefits for gay partners, which made us, in Bob's words, "the devil's airline."

We are all just trying to get through this thing called life the best we know how. Some people may think that they know the better route. It's fine to share your thoughts, but to cast aspersions and spoil another's path is wrong. To all of you who have met a Bible Bob along the way and have turned yourself off to religion because of that person, please try again. Religion can be, and is, a truly wonderful thing.

The C E Uh Oh

Who are these men and women holding the title of Chief Executive Officer that head up American companies of today? How do they get the job, and who arranges their ridiculous pay packages? They bask in the glory when their company reports stellar profits, but hide in the shadows when earnings come in short. For the past few years, corporate America has been seeing tough times, and while scandal after scandal is being discovered, little or nothing is being done about fraud at the top.

Heaven forbid they should ever be asked to resign or the company goes out of business. I was shocked when the airline I previously worked for closed its doors. The company didn't have enough money to pay the employees' last paychecks or for the fuel to get their airplanes back home, but they did have enough to pay off the golden parachutes for the top brass. While the employees scrambled for their pensions, the fat cats at the top got paid first and foremost.

According to a recent author and former CEO, the practice of monetarily rewarding the people in charge is the only way to get quality personnel. I say hogwash. Give them their reward in the form of stock options and provide direct incentive. If they perform and do the job as they claim they can, then their bonus is well-deserved, but if the company goes into bankruptcy protection, let them share in the pain like everyone else. Make it a win-lose situation, not a win-win.

The president of the United States, earning $400,000 a year, makes a tenth of what most CEOs of major corporations are making these days. Match their salaries with his. All too often, you hear CEOs say, "Oh, well, I tried; that will be three million dollars, please." In the business world today, we are starting to see the people in charge held responsible for their compensation packages and perks, but this is only the beginning. More has to be done and people should not merely shrug it off as, "They're the ones with all the power, what are you going to do?" First of all, go to the stockholders' meetings. If you don't own stock, buy one share and by law you have a right to attend. Voice your opinion, write letters, run for a Union seat, do something other than merely complain to your friends.

What I find completely ludicrous is that during these times of economic hardship the airlines are asking for financial assistance from the federal government. All the while airline CEOs are raking in some of their biggest bonuses ever. I don't know about you, but I am not inclined to give money to a panhandler in a pin-stripe suit. I say kudos to the government for investigating this particular subject more closely.

There is a certain airline that has changed CEOs more times than the seat cushions. Each time they do, they lose millions in retirement packages. It's no wonder they are now in a deep financial crisis. It is like my dad who married seven times. He was wealthy with his first wife, and broke by the seventh. The airline continues to pay alimony to former CEOs in the form of compensation packages. You would think the salaries would get smaller as the company's financial situation worsens. Not so; they just get more complicated, adding safeguards if the company goes out of business.

Suppose I were asked to be the new CEO of a struggling airline. I can fantasize how I would negotiate a contract. My wife and I would gather by the fire with a bottle of red wine. We would get a pen and paper and make a list of the most outrageous demands, giggling all the while.

1. Multi-million-dollar signing bonus.
2. Free First Class for life.
3. Hotel suite at the Ritz whenever and wherever desired.
4. Annual multi-million-dollar salary.
5. Golden retirement package.
6. Safeguard clauses ensuring all benefits should the company go out of business.
7. If I resign, get fired, or am forced out, I would be guaranteed full and immediate compensation.

You may think I am exaggerating, but this is unfortunately the standard salary package for today's major airline CEOs. I haven't even mentioned such perks as stock options and ritzy golf club memberships. This doesn't sound like a struggling airline to me.

If the board of directors approved my appointment as CEO, my first point of business would be to fire everyone responsible for agreeing to such a ridiculous contract. When the CEO claims to feel the pain while slicing up every employee's paycheck, I want to know where his pain derives from. Is it his guilty conscience? My advice to the people at the top: try not to overdo the lavish gifts and First Class treatment; realize that many people rely on you to be fair and to return their company to profitable times; and when you say you feel the pain, really feel it, or at least do a better job pretending.

Shame on those of you at the top who are getting away with robbery while you reduce the checks of your front-line workers! And while you laugh your way to the bank, you'd better hope there is no such thing as karma, because your employees are betting on it.

The Sogranos

Suppose you have just started a new job. Someone in a business suit approaches you with a smile and an enthusiastic "Welcome to the company!" He then tells you that he wants to protect you from the bad guys, your employer, or any outside elements you may encounter on the job. You will pay him a predetermined monthly fee for these services, and your choice is limited to pay or no work.

You have to admit it sounds like organized crime and the protection rackets of the old days. Well, that's what you're confronted with when you join an airline with a union. Of course, you have a choice — you can pay the money and not be a member of the union, or you can pay and be a member. Either way, you pay. That doesn't sound like much of a choice to me. Many unions can raise their dues as they see fit, and, while you do have a say, they don't have to listen to you.

Now, don't get me wrong, I feel that unions in general are an important aspect of obtaining beneficial rules and adequate compensation. I just don't like being collectively forced into a situation. Also, since they have my monthly dues regardless of their performance, what motivation do they have to work harder? Well, one might argue that they can get voted out. Pretty much any smart union has made it practically impossible to be removed. The few attempted coups almost always fall by the wayside.

Have you ever been on a flight and noticed a flight attendant reading a small booklet? If it's not the in-flight handbook, odds are it is their employment contract and they are looking up some type of work rule or legality. The main purpose of the union is to establish and enforce a good contract with fair work rules and compensation. This is one of the main ways of keeping the airlines honest. I can't stress the importance of the contract enough, as I know what it is like to work without one.

It never occurred to me to write a chapter like this until one day an elderly lady from my union approached me. She was a bit overweight, with graying hair and a raspy voice from years of smoking. Maybe I have seen too many mafia movies, but she was the female version of The Godfather's Marlon Brando.

"So, Frankie, I hear you like to write little airline stories?"

"Uh, yeah, sort of, why?" I replied.

"If you ever write one about the union, just remember what side your bread is buttered. Got it?"

I chuckled to myself and thought of a bizarre version of The Sopranos. A bunch of elderly ladies sitting around a table mafioso style. They are knitting, playing bridge, and sipping sherry.

"So, Betty, what are we going to do about this Frankie Steward character?" the Godmother says as she pops her daily vitamins.

"Shall I fit him for a concrete life vest?" Betty answers.

"No, not yet, let me give him the old buttered bread lecture."

The irony to this is that if I get in trouble for writing this book, the very people I am ridiculing in this chapter are the ones who will help me keep my job. Hopefully, they have a sense of humor as well. If not, I will say hello to Jimmy Hoffa for everyone, or at least take a number in the unemployment office.

Silicon Valley

Working in a predominately female-oriented career, I have been given an insight into the other half. I get the inside scoop on what makes women tick, their likes and dislikes, and I am privy to conversations in which I would normally not be included. I am a good listener, married, and not considered to be a "threatening male type," so, often I am called upon for a man's opinion. I will answer just about any question, and I never cease to be surprised at what women ask me.

In the flight attendant arena there is a well-known phenomenon called "the jumpseat syndrome." No matter how little you may have in common with a fellow crewmember, once you sit down on a jumpseat, everything, including personal life details, seems to easily flow. On the basis of numerous discussions over the years, I am sure that nine out of 10 women under the age of 40 has contemplated or had breast augmentation at some time or another. Breasts are as important to a woman as the hairline is to a man. In the flight attendant pay scale there is a considerable jump after the fifth year. I'll give you one guess what many buy themselves at that time.

When asked for my opinion, I respond cautiously, knowing they may already have made up their mind or have had augmentation already. In my opinion, you should keep what you have, unless your chest is noticeably flat or for medical reasons. Variety is the spice of life, and the same goes for the chest. With all the breast augmentation taking place today, the variety is starting to diminish.

Men these days prefer the real thing and find augmentation a turn-off. Sometimes the procedure goes wrong and seepage or scarring occurs. In addition, women risk the loss of some sensation in that area. One flight attendant after having the operation didn't look bustier; instead she appeared fat. Many women claim they hate being stared at as a sex object, but don't such operations encourage those kinds of leers?

If you are interested in augmentation, do it for yourself and nobody else. If you believe it will improve your self-esteem, ask someone with a large chest if it is all that it is cracked up to be. Just make sure you are clear about what motivates you.

One time I was flying with a sweet flight attendant named Sherry, who, although she appreciated my opinion on the matter, did not agree with me. We met out at the pool and continued our debate until she got annoyed and removed her bikini top to prove her point. She had a completely flat chest. Not that she needed my approval, but she did make her case, and became one of the exceptions to my rule. She had the operation, her bust is not too big, and she looks wonderful. I find it amusing that when many of my friends get the operation, they want a man's opinion about the results and oftentimes show me. Mind you, I am not complaining — I always wanted to be a breast examiner!

As far as men and their hairline go, I can't be much help there. Most men who start to lose their hair follow the new trend of cutting it all off. While it may work well for some, it is not an option for me. My nickname in the military after having my head shaved was "Watermelon Head," so you can see the conflict of interest there. I fly with men who try the oh-so-noticeable toupee, the comb-over, and even a pilot who doesn't fool anyone with the spray-on hair.

Many male crewmembers go to South America in search of cheaper minoxydil products or miracle lotions. A close friend of mine thinks he has found the answer to baldness in crushing up birth control pills and massaging them into his scalp. I am not sure what I will do when I lose my hair, but would rather not resort to taking my wife's medication. Maybe by then my back hair would have grown sufficiently for me to start a new trend of comb-over. As they say, hair today, gone tomorrow.

Insecurity Revisited

My first book, *The Air Traveler's Survival Guide*, was released on September 10, one day before the terrorist events of 9/11. In the chapter "Insecurity" I stated that America's airports were a terrorist activity waiting to happen. Unfortunately, the unthinkable happened and now flying will never be the same again. I am not sorry that I said it, as it was a feeling shared by many airline employees.

Some people say airport security isn't any better than before the tragedy; I strongly disagree. Air travel is safer now than it has ever been. I used to be appalled that airline employees were never screened. Now, nearly everyone is. It used to scare me that bags would go on a domestic flight regardless of whether the owner was on the plane. Airlines now have a 100% bag match rule, which, although it is causing a few delays, is being strictly enforced. I used to think up ways of getting items past security; those ways are now 75% gone. Every day brings new methods of heightened security, from closer shoe inspection to high-tech machines. America and its airline industry cannot afford to have a repeat terrorist incident. So everything possible is being done to prevent such events.

Okay, having said all of that, there are some hassles along the way. First and foremost, the lines at security are probably enough to turn you right off of air travel. In my case, I know that the shortest distance between two points is not the line that I seem to choose. I always get close to the front and something gets clogged up, and all the other lines move. Then, as I switch lines, the new one gets jammed and the one I left starts moving. I believe there are certain tricks of the trade that can get you through a bit more quickly and comfortably. The following are some Frank tips to help you through the new airport security procedures:

1. Put any sharp objects or any electrical devices you don't need on the flight into your checked luggage. Checked luggage is not accessible during the flight, so certain items are scrutinized considerably less.

2. Remove anything from your person that is remotely metallic, such as jewelry, watches, coins, etc., and put them in your carry-on bag that goes through the x-ray machine. This way, you won't set off the metal detector or forget any item you put in the plastic tray.

3. Pick a line and stick to it. Bring a book — better yet, bring my book — to pass the time.

4. Walk through the metal detector in one brisk stride. Stopping half way, or walking through slowly, often causes false alarms.

5. Ladies, if you see a line of men queuing for the metal detector, be aware that screeners are now gender specific. Odds are high that there is a female screener waiting for a female passenger. Walk up to the front and get noticed.

6. If you are a frequent traveler and keep setting off the metal detector, listen and pay attention as the screener wands you. If your buttons trigger the alarm, next time wear different attire. Ladies, try to avoid bras with under-wire support. The next time you fly you will know what to avoid wearing.

7. Watch your carry-on items when you are being waved with the security wand. Even with the added officials and video surveillance technology, they can still be an opportunity for thieves.

8. Don't cause a scene. I know it's frustrating to be singled out, but that tantrum you are about to throw could delay your journey over 30 minutes. They will send you through every level of security checks they have, just on principle.

9. Please don't get mad at the airline crews when we go to the front of the line. How would you like to discover the reason for your flight delay was that the crew was held up at security?

10. Speak up and be Frank! I have said it before and I will say it again: If you witness a breach of security, tell someone immediately. Apparently, one day in August prior to the tragedy, a well-known actor had witnessed a breach of security involving a man at Boston's Logan Airport. He spoke up, but nothing was done. Later, authorities determined that the man was one of the 9/11 hijackers doing a practice run. They will listen to you now, I guarantee it. The life you save may be yours, but it may be mine as well.

Unspoken Heroes

A hero is defined as anyone who has displayed great courage or exceptionally noble qualities. Everyone has their own definitions and ideas of what makes a hero. Lance Armstrong comes to my mind for his ability to overcome cancer and win the Tour de France time and time again. Others reserve the word for our military men and women who fight when their country calls. A hero can be anyone from a boy who helps his grandmother, to a person who risks his life while saving another.

The 9/11 atrocity produced countless heroes. The firefighters, police, bystanders, and even politicians responded with great heroism. Some of these brave people became victims but remain heroes, regardless. America as a nation reacted heroically.

I want to tell you about a group of lesser-known heroes--flight attendants and pilots. On September 11, flight crews

207

watched the events unfold with the rest of the world. They then listened with horror as the graphic details of their flying partners' demise were revealed. They learned that their colleagues were the first to die. Some of the flight attendants were brutally murdered as a form of crowd coercion and as a way to lure the pilots out of the cockpit.

All over the world flights were grounded as flight crews tried to reassure passengers even when they were unsure themselves. They went out on layovers and tried to help in any way they could. Many looked up into the sky, saw no airplanes, and cried. Fearing for their co-workers and country, they stood by as their airlines told them to be ready to fly.

After the tragedy, the public didn't want to get back on an airplane; flight crews had to. They now feared for their jobs, their airline's future, and their lives. Many pondered giving up and quitting. They were scared to board an aircraft again, but when it was time, they did just that. The flight attendants armed themselves with ice mallets and played out repeat scenarios in their minds. The pilots barricaded themselves in the cockpit, mentally flinching any time they heard a knock on the door or the in-flight phone ring. Flight crews now have attended, and continue to attend, an endless amount of classes--from self-defense to new security procedures--that only serves to remind them of the fate of their fallen colleagues. Fear is now, and will always be, a major part of their job and lifestyle. Many updated their wills and sought therapy, searching for an answer from within. Some found the answers while many others are still looking.

The heroes which stand out from that horrible day may not include the ones who you considered courageous, but I believe the hero is in the eye of the beholder. For the flight attendants and pilots who got back on an airplane and continue to fly, you are truly heroes.

Terminal 6

Time for Landing

Memory Lane

Having the benefit of free air travel, I have the luxury of visiting the places of my past at will. Time has a way of ironing out the rough bits and making wonderful memories. Going through some boxes one summer, I came across an old address book that had to be at least 15 years old. I was curious whether any of the addresses or numbers were still valid. As I turned the pages, some names I winced at and at others I smiled. I had always intended to stroll down Memory Lane, but until that point, the only wandering in the past had been in my mind.

I picked up the phone and started dialing. Some phone numbers were still good and others led me to new ones. I talked to a variety of people from dear to not so dear friends; I even talked to an old high school teacher. Why? Because the numbers were in the book and maybe the boredom of the day was turning into sweet nostalgia. Out of the whole address book, I had made arrangements to meet up with three people from the past — an old army buddy, an ex-girlfriend from Germany, and a best friend from elementary school.

The army buddy turned out to be worn out on life. His family was not only a drag mentally, but he had to work all the time to keep his four girls in private school. He only wanted to talk about women, he was a raging alcoholic, and his bald head and aged exterior just made me realize how old I was becoming.

The ex-girlfriend was married, but so was I, and this was purely a friendly meeting. On a layover in Germany, I took the train four hours away to see her. She was an important part of my past. She taught me the German language. I was 18 years old and she was 30, so, needless to say, she taught me a different language as well. After the hug, hello, and the "It's really great to see you," we sat down to a glass of wine. In the course of ten minutes she managed to bitch me out about:

1. Why I hadn't called for so long.
2. How bad my German was.
3. The audacity of me expecting her to drop everything because I was in town.
4. How I offended her husband by not inviting him.
5. The exact nature of my visit after so many years.

I realized then, albeit too late, why I had ended contact and exactly why we broke up. I couldn't stand her. Time didn't change this, but it did bring back the rushing feelings of inadequacy she had always seemed to instill in me. After the meal, I made a kind escape, managing to avoid giving my contact number or address. I paid the bill and she stated that next time her husband and my wife should join us. I smiled politely and said, "Next time? Right," knowing full well that there would be no next time.

I was wary about meeting up with my best friend from elementary school. The other two meetings hadn't gone as planned, so I hoped the third one might be a charm. My friend was from a perfect family — a great mom and dad, a beautiful sister whom I always had a crush on, and the most wonderful of family atmospheres. I came from the classic dysfunctional family, so throughout the years I had always known they took pity on me. It didn't matter in the slightest.

The directions to his house were familiar, as I soon discovered that he still lived at home with his father. Over the first beer I found out that his mother had run away and joined a cult. His sister was a manic depressive lesbian. His dad wouldn't accept the daughter, thus they rarely spoke, and my friend was bitter on life, recently returning from his third drug rehabilitation center. The functional family had become extremely dysfunctional, and, while it made my situation seem more normal, I didn't like the feeling that my past was starting to crumble.

The stroll down Memory Lane was over. In my mind, my army buddy wasn't the fun-loving guy of old. My ex-girlfriend was now, as before, a nagging, spiteful lady, and my classic functional family was really a closet dysfunctional family. My memories were now tainted and all I could hope for was that in time those wrinkles would iron out as well.

You know the old saying, "You can never go back?" Maybe the more appropriate saying is, "Sometimes you *should* never go back."

I now believe that some strolls down this lane should take place only in the mind, where mostly the fond memories remain.

The Nightmare Neighbor

I had thought of everything, as I sat down for the cross-country four-hour flight. I had earplugs, music, writing pad, a snack if I didn't like the food aboard, and I even had a couple miniatures of my favorite liquor, just in case. I was a savvy flyer and had all the controllable variables covered. The uncontrollable variables include airplane mechanical status, delays, cancellations, and other passengers, of which you just have to hope for the best.

My seat neighbor was a man in his early forties who appeared harmless at first glance. I was lucky enough to get a roomy seat in the exit row. Since I am a Virgo and extremely aware of my surroundings, a seat neighbor can make or break a flight for me. The ticking of a clock, small noises, or constant rattle will also have me climbing the walls after a while; thus I never leave home without earplugs.

After take-off, I discovered that my seat partner was a multi-tasker of troubles. He later explained he was a claustrophobic with Parkinson's and Tourette's. He cleared his throat every ten seconds, and let out some mild profanity every three to five minutes, all the while his left hand trembled.

Now, please believe me when I say that I was sympathetic. I felt sorry for this person and his problems, so I did my best to relax and avoid letting the situation get to me. I turned on my MP3 player to full volume, closed my eyes, and thought of some faraway place. I could feel his shaking, so I incorporated it into the fantasy place that I was trying to hide in. It was a good practice for me in self-control and patience.

Once in a while, I would open my eyes and see the passengers around me look over in frustration and shock at some of his outbursts. I was going to need my drink reserve. I was positive I was sitting next to a mental case, and I am sure he thought he was sitting next to an alcoholic. He smiled at me, clenched his fists, and yelled, "Asshole!"

"How are you doing, sir? Is there anything I can help you with?" I asked in search of some official medical explanation.

"I'm fine, and I am sorry you got stuck next to me." He popped a pill from his bag, and proceeded to tell me of his ailments. His name was Ray, and his condition was not only a problem he had, but also a problem the public had with him. He was traveling with a group of 20 people, but they specifically requested to sit away from him. This is a bit sneaky because airline rules do state that people with his condition must have someone traveling with them, but the rules don't specify that they have to sit next to him. He had a connecting flight to Australia, which was a further 14 hours.

The more I talked with Ray, the more I grew to like him. He used his illnesses as a focal point for observation and learned a lot about people from their reactions. It was the kind of social mandate I had set for myself, but mine was from a fade-in-the-background approach, while his condition commanded attention. He could probably write a book based solely on how he was treated by others.

At one point in the conversation, a male passenger in the row in front of us started to yell at the flight attendant about the poor service and meal quality.

"Watch this," Ray said. "Asshole!" The man stopped, turned, and ceased his temper tantrum. Every time the man would attempt to start his tirade, he got an earful.

The flight attendant, while appearing shocked, also had a gleam in her eye when she glanced at Ray, as if to say "Thank you."

"You see, everything has its advantages. So I have been dealt a couple of lemons." Ray looked on the bright side of his ailments. His claustrophobia got him the extra roomy seats in the Economy cabin, and the Parkinson's disease rocked him to sleep at night. He really did have Tourette's, but occasionally faked an outburst at will. Could you imagine a flight attendant with Tourette's? That would be interesting, to say the least. His condition didn't seem all that noticeable after a while.

I admired Ray's outlook and felt lucky to have met him. He told me he was currently looking for a wife, but realized it was going to be hard to find a woman willing to put up with all of his lemons. I told him I was sure she was out there somewhere, and suggested a Gemini or a Taurus, but to stay way clear of Virgos.

The Wong Impression

The place I go to get my haircut is also where my wife gets her nails done. They do a decent enough job and there is comfort in not always having to explain how I like my hair cut. The Wong family runs the place and everyone who works there is very friendly.

I discovered them while quietly waiting for my wife to get her nails done.

"That you husband?" Mrs. Wong, the woman working on my wife's nails, asked in a thick Oriental accent.

My wife nodded discreetly.

"He cute but he have big size head," she said loud enough that everyone in the waiting room, including myself, over-heard. I looked up in mild disbelief.

She smiled at me and said, "Means you have more brain, very wise. But also means you have wrong haircut."

That was enough for me, so I became their new customer. There was something delightful in their lack of tact. While some might find it offensive, Martha and I found it refreshing. There was no putting on airs or beating around the bush. If something was in question, she would ask. "Why you no eat meat? You too thin. You not one of those wussy boys, are you?" I usually responded with a laugh.

Even when it was too personal, like with Martha, "Why your ear stick out like that?" Now, nobody makes fun of that ear, not even me. Somehow, the questions would never hit us the wrong way and we would always be in hysterics when we left.

After the 9/11 attacks, life was depressing. There was not much to laugh about. We were tired of the media updates, memorials, and friends who tiptoed past sensitive topics of conversation. Martha and I went into the Wongs' salon for our normal grooming services. We expected a reserved conversation, as was the case with most people in our circle of life.

"I bet you glad you not in one of those plane that crashed, huh?" It was the first question out of their mouths. Not, how are you coping? Or, are you all right? No, it was dive right in head first.

"Yes, I am thankful," I replied.

She looked at my wife and said, "What about you, you look so sad. You very lucky too."

"Actually, I just got laid off from my job," Martha replied.

"Oh, that's okay, you need to take it easy, take a vacation, lose some weight, you be fine."

"The whole terrorism aspect is a bit hard to grasp, don't you think?" I interjected, trying to steer the conversation away from the last remark.

"Look, I no be uncaring, September 11th was truly awful day. But what people don't think about, it has been happening all over world and for all time. Few examples, Dresden, Germany was bombed by England and American forces and 50,000 people died overnight. In Asia my mother and father were killed right in front of my brother and me. Trung, the cashier, was only one to survive from his village in Viet Nam War. What about the bombs in Hiroshima and Nagasaki? Whatever don't kill you make you stronger, and America getting stronger already. It like Oprah say, don't sweat small stuff, and all of it, small stuff." Martha and I sat silently, as we digested a very good point.

Somehow, they always managed to cheer us up, even though every other comment could be construed as an insult — wussy boy, lose weight, big head, etc. One topic of conversation that kept surfacing which Martha avoided was the child issue. It started to annoy her so we decided to zing Mrs. Wong with a fib the next time she asked. Sure enough, the next visit she let out, "Why you no have kids?" Martha quickly answered back, "Well, we are not sure we are able to."

We waited for a reaction, or maybe a little embarrassment, but without skipping a beat she replied, "Ah, you very lucky, kids are pain in ass anyway."

Martha and I attended Mrs. Wong's celebration of U.S. citizenship. Her wide ear-to-ear smile brought joy to everyone's heart. She insisted on singing the national anthem to everyone at the party. Everyone smiled and listened contentedly, and, while we didn't recognize many of the words due to her thick accent, Martha and I tried desperately not to laugh. Afterwards everyone applauded, laughed, and remarked how awful and off-key she was, in a fun-loving way. We couldn't believe how honest but caring everyone was. It was great to see their traditional lack of tact was not just a tradition at work but in their personal life as well. I like to look on it as their way of being Frank.

"Pretty horrible, huh? Remember, all small stuff." Mrs. Wong winked at us as she passed. I don't think the smile left her face all evening.

It was the cutest rendition of the national anthem I have ever heard and sung by a true patriot. America has a new citizen and we are all very lucky to have her.

A Grand Lesson

My grandfather, Franklin Sr., worked for a major newspaper back in the days of scoops, vodka in the coffee cups, and unfiltered cigarettes. He worked his way up to the top job of senior editor. All of his friends and co-workers around him were starting a disturbing trend of retiring at age 65 and dying soon after. It became so predictable that instead of looking forward to retiring, most were fearful. As 65 was the mandatory retirement age, there was no alternative and their fear was pointless. They would preface it as, "Maybe it will be different this time." Most of the time it wasn't.

My grandfather was 60 when he made editor. His best friend had recently retired and died a week later. It was that one event which caused Franklin Sr. to make a huge decision. Even though it would mean a 50% cut in his pension and a considerable strain on his retirement years, he did the unthinkable at the time and retired early. He hung up his typewriter and whisked my grandmother away on a world tour. They bought a VW van in Germany and drove all over Europe. Then they headed to South America and trekked in the Andes Mountains. Afterwards they explored Australia and lived in New Zealand for a year. For several years they discovered the lands my grandfather had only written about and my grandmother had always taught about in school.

At 8 a.m. the day after my grandfather's 65th birthday he passed away. I was only a small boy when he died, and didn't really know him as a person, but he taught me the biggest lesson of my life: Enjoy life while you can; it's no good worrying too much if you won't be around to enjoy it.

My grandmother always smiled when she told of their adventures. She cherished her photo albums and went through them every time we visited. They had never once regretted their choice of early retirement. One day she let me in on a little secret. They had, in her words, "made whoopie" the night before he died and she always feared that it might have been too much for him. Okay, I know the thought of your grandparents being intimate isn't the best of thoughts, but I do know what I want from my wife on my 65th birthday (knock on wood).

Thirty years later my grandmother joined my grandfather. They were, and still are, my ideal picture of love and endurance. I am sure they are out there somewhere playing gin rummy, laughing and making up for lost time.

I wonder if Franklin Sr. would have been proud of me. I am doing a combination of what he liked best – writing and traveling. While I do hope to retire at age 55, I am not so sure I will be able to. If anyone wishes to help, please give generously to the H.M.R.E. (Help Me Retire Early) fund. Or at least keep buying my books.

My point in all of this is to say, don't let life get away from you with out enjoying the better part. Let the future take care of itself; enjoy the now before it's history and so are you.

Be Franklin, so to speak.

What a Bore

I have eaten all over the world and have tried just about every entrée on the menu of each country visited. I have sampled snake in Asia and feasted on cow brains in Russia. I am not a vegetarian. I don't have special dietary restrictions and have a fairly open mind when it comes to trying new delicacies. So when the chef in Brussels recommended the "wild boar in a creamy mushroom sauce," I did not hesitate, although I was a bit curious about how one comes across fresh wild boar in Belgium. If it was raised on a farm, wouldn't that just make it a boar without the "wild"?

While the sauce was delicious, the meat was a bit tough and gamy but, being hungry, I cleaned my plate, adding "wild boar" to my list of consumed exotic entrees on layovers.

Upon my return home, I was to be off the next few days

226

and had millions of chores to do, but the following morning I had a mild case of diarrhea and a slight chill. It was November so I deduced I was coming down with the flu. By the end of the day my posterior region was itching. While not exactly life threatening, any irritation in that area is an unpleasant experience. At three in the morning I awoke with severe chills and a burning bottom that I wanted to rub sandpaper all over in order to relieve the unbearable itch.

My wife woke up from my constant tossing and turning, and asked if there was anything she could do to help. Now, I used to think "true love" was holding hands in the park, hugging, and saying "I love you" all the time. No, true love to me now is a middle-aged man bent over in the bathroom in the wee hours of the morning, with an extremely sympathetic wife.

We tried creams, baths, and home remedies but nothing helped. The next day my condition subsided a bit, and I did an Internet search, finding some pretty good medical websites.

An hour later I had the following possible diagnosis: diabetes, cancer, or parasites (pin or tape worms). The one question that clinched it was, "Has the patient eaten anything unusual or been to a foreign country recently?" Bingo! I had done both. My next mistake was looking up the various causes and effects of parasitic infection. The pictures alone were enough to scare me to death. I turned the computer off and worriedly smirked, trying to convince myself that my condition was improving. I thought about calling the pilot on my Brussels crew who had also eaten the "wild boar," but how would I phrase it? "Hey, Bob, your butt been itching lately?"

Nighttime came again and my condition was twice as bad as the night before. It seemed like an eternity until morning.

I called my doctor's office first thing, and, of course, the sweet young secretary asked, "What seems to be the problem?"

"Well, um, uh...I have sort of a condition."

"And what would that be?" she prodded.

"Uh, I have an intense case of ...posterior itch."

"Anal itching!" she announced to the world.

After I explained that it might be worms and I couldn't wait three days for an appointment, she squeezed me into the schedule the next day and told me to bring a stool sample. Aw, now, how was I going to do that? I nervously pondered.

Another restless night passed. I went into the doctor's office with my wife by my side and my special package tucked deep into my coat pocket. I brought my wife for security, support, and to avoid suspicion that would come from being a male flight attendant and having complications in that part of the body.

The waiting room was full, so when the secretary asked for the stool sample you could have heard a pin drop as everyone stopped and stared. I made it into the examination room and after being bent over for 15 minutes, the doctor mumbling with flashlight in hand, and the nurse opening and closing the door, I began to feel like a window display. My wife declared it was payback for all her visits to her gynecologist. The lab test was negative for parasites so the doctor began with some basic questions. In the end, no pun intended, the culprit was a new scented brand of toilet paper that my wife had recently purchased. It had caused an allergic reaction. How boaring is that?

A little cortisone, another brand of toilet paper, and I returned to normal a few days later. Although my appetite for wild boar never returned, I learned two important things from the episode:

1. As I grow older I will undoubtedly find myself in worse situations, and the human body is nothing to be embarrassed about. "It's the greatest instrument I will ever own."

2. Hypochondriacs should stay well away from the Internet!

It's an episode that I can laugh at now, but one that I wish I could wipe from my memory, preferably with the unscented kind.

Booking Variety

My wife and I were in shock when we moved into a bigger house. Overnight we went from a living space of 1,000 square feet to 5,000. A warning to all men: When a woman asks, "How are we going to fill all this space up?" she probably already knows.

It had a spacious library with built-in mahogany bookshelves that would accommodate over a thousand books. The problem was that we only had about 50 books to our name. We both loved to read, but never saw the point in keeping a book once it was read.

One night we came up with a plan. After every flight, we would scan the airplane for books left behind and bring them home. On average, there were two books on smaller planes and three or four on larger ones.

Slowly but surely, we began filling our empty shelves. Since we worked for an international airline, the variety was quite extreme. We would hold no prejudices. If it was a book and left behind, then it went on our shelves. On one flight I found eight books — the standing record so far.

Now the library is full, and the variety offers quite a conversation piece for guests. The shelves contain everything from Kurt Vonnegut to saucy romance novels, Buddhism to speaking Hebrew. I even picked up the Spanish version of *The Joy of Sex*. Mind you, one has to be quite discreet reading books of such content on an airplane.

I find myself reading books that I never would have thought twice about. Some of them are fascinating, while others are marginal, but they have opened my mind up to the world's diversity. Have you ever read a book and expected not to like it, only to be thoroughly entertained? I now have approximately nine hundred books just waiting to be read.

Have you ever left a book on an airplane and wondered what happened to it? You never know, it may be on my shelves right now. I always wonder if I will ever find one that I wrote. What would it mean? Where would the pages be dog-eared? Did the reader like it?

Even though my library is now full, I am still in the habit of bringing stray books home. I place them into boxes in the basement, with the intent of reading each and every one of them when I retire. Maybe I will learn Spanish and be able to translate *The Joy of Sex* to my wife by then.

Next time you are on a plane and find a book, no matter what it's about or what it looks like, give it a try. Someone else went to great hardship writing, publishing, and even buying that book. As we all know, we should never judge a book by its cover.

The Mooner's Gang

I never saw myself as the "marrying type." My father had set a family record of seven marriages, my longest previous relationship was a day shy of six months, and my firm belief was that "true love" did not exist in the modern world. Luckily, Martha came along and proved me wrong. She and I married in England in the non-traditional month of January. We had met January 23rd, got engaged January 23rd the next year, and hence married on the same date the following year. The way I figured it, I had three of the "must not forget" dates covered on one day. If I forgot that date, then I was a lost cause indeed!

Her family was responsible for the wedding, and I planned the honeymoon. Since we had been living together for approximately two years prior, I decided that the typical honeymoon of lying on some tropical deserted beach, wondering if we had done the "right thing" was not for us.

Instead, considering the time of year, we chose to escape to the Swiss Alps for an exciting ski trip. I rented a chalet in the mountains and did the unthinkable: I invited nine of our closest friends to come along! We had been swamped with obstacles prior to saying "I do." With her parents not approving of my career and my family being spread across the globe with no contact for years, we decided to keep the party going and celebrate the legalization of our love with our closest friends.

The wedding was magical, but the honeymoon was incredible. The Alps had received its best snowfall in 20 years, but more importantly we had gathered the finest group of characters we ever could have hoped for. We had fondue every night, drank too much, and partied with people we met on the slopes. We enjoyed life for the moment, the way it's supposed to be enjoyed. Never in our wildest dreams could we have planned a more perfect conclusion to a hectic build-up of clashing families and emotions. The best part about it was Martha and I were going to spend the rest of our lives with each other's best friend and "true love."

We were sad to see the honeymoon end, but anxious to discover the joys and perils of marriage. Each of the nine people who had joined us expressed an interest in a repeat performance the following year. We complied and planned another ski vacation in a different part of the world, thus beginning the tradition of the "Mooner's."

We all had "free travel" benefits; we were young and adventurous, with no signs of boundaries on the horizon. Year after year, we ventured to different parts of the world and congregated for friendship and fun. The rules were that the original nine were lifetime members and each could invite one person to the next trip, and so on. We started by renting ski-side mansions but when we reached 25 plus, we realized separate accommodations were needed.

All the characters there ranged from the swinging single to the happily married, the exhibitionist to the cheap guy who never bought a round. We were based all around the world, and while it was rare to meet up on a flight, we could always count on the Mooner's vacation to bring us all together. We went from Canada to Colorado, and Europe to Japan. If the skiing was good, we were blessed; if it wasn't, then we had more time to enjoy one another. There was no such thing as a bad Mooner's trip.

Even though we grew older, some left the airline, and others had children, still, nothing got in the way of our trips. It is important to make time in life for your friends, as they are what memories are made of. It is said that when you grow older, you should narrow the geographic gap between yourself and your friends. While this isn't possible for the members of our group, one week a year suffices quite nicely.

If you are interested in joining us or just looking for new friends, we always have room. Go to www.franksteward .com and click the Mooner's link. Our motto is "We are drinkers with a skiing problem, and life is taken way too seriously."

When It Rains, It Pours

The stage was set: bankruptcy was looming over our heads, liquidation rumors in every newspaper article, fuel prices soaring, the Gulf War Part 2 minutes from commencing, future bookings taking a nose dive, vultures hovering overhead hoping for the best bits of our airline, European flights suffering from the antiwar sentiment of America's allies, and a mystery virus in Asia cautioning against all unnecessary travel. To top it all off, our management was threatening to discard the work rules that took more than 20 years to build. All in all, it was a gloomy forecast, and the future wasn't promising.

It was spring and I had decided to pick up an easy two-day trip to Denver. If I have learned anything in life, it is that nothing is as easy as it seems; this was no exception. The night I arrived, the beautiful white flakes that I had recently learned to despise fell lightly as I entered the hotel.

The next morning, I boarded the crew bus to well over a foot of snow, yet the crew desk assured us that the airplanes were scheduled on time. Yes, they use that line on us as well.

We got to the airport and the canceled signs had taken the place of every departure time. This was the last thing our airline or the crewmembers needed. I had suffered through the worst East Coast winter in decades, but now it was 70 degrees back home and I was a canceled 3,000-mile flight away. The flight crews gathered for their new assignments. Four hours later, I received a hotel voucher to go back to the hotel I had started the day from. I joined the growing number of crewmembers outside waiting for the hotel transportation. One small van arrived every 15 minutes, barely making a dent in the waiting lines. There were at least 200 employees in front of me and the snow started to fall at a feverish rate. There was talk of having the stranded employees sleep on the parked airplanes, but I needed a hot shower, so I stood fast. My only form of comic relief stemmed from watching 50 employees cram into a 20-capacity van. The realization that this was what I was in line for swiftly erased my smirk.

Three islands of crowds formed. One for the taxicabs (that eventually stopped arriving), another for the disgruntled and inconvenienced passengers waiting for the hotel buses, and ours, the stranded crewmembers. Once in a while some of the passengers would yell at us or cross over and complain, as if we were responsible for the weather. We just turned our backs, holding back with all of our might what we would have liked to have said. It was like a gathering of gangs getting ready to rumble.

It was truly a mixed crowd of employees. The Florida crews, not expecting a stay in Denver, were caught without their winter wear. The mothers on the one-day trips were worried about their babysitters, and the pilots were glued to their cell phones. Once in a while I ran into a few friendly faces whom I hadn't seen since training, but the atmosphere was strained, as you could just tell that the worry about our airline's future was on everyone's mind.

The snow started to fall so heavily that the scene became ridiculous. At which point a male flight attendant unpacked a portable music player and started playing the radio, providing some audio relief. A popular song came on that had the reoccurring theme of "I want to be somebody else." It was funny at first, as everyone could really relate to the words. It then became eerily profound as people started to sing along and wiggle to the beat. Everyone, including the pilots, got into the spirit. It wasn't pretty or pleasing to the ears, and we must have looked like a bunch of lunatics to the other people, but it felt wonderful. I normally hate musicals, but this was the closest I have come to being in one, and I loved it.

It was freezing, our future was gloomy, but we were all in it together and grooving in the diversion of the moment. Sometimes in life, the best thing to do is let go of all your worries, and just dance.

Tomorrow is always a new day.

(Okay, the airport roof collapsed, we were stuck in Denver for five days, and the Gulf War Part 2 began, but you get the point.)

Diary of A. Frank

By an Irish Stew

My name is Frank the airline Stew.
Flying the skies, here to serve you.
Going places some never see.
Best thing about it, I get there for free.

Arrive at work, meet up with the crew.
Discuss our layover and what we will do.
Start at the pool, lay in the sun,
Cocktails at six, it's gonna be fun.

Finished with briefing we get on the plane.
Sometimes the boarding can be such a pain.
Bag after bag, "What did you pack?"
"Can you lift my suitcase? I've got a bad back."

238

All are aboard, we push from the gate.
Now to tell you, we've a two-hour wait.
Question is now will you make your next flight?
"Will I make my connection?" "It's going to be tight."

After a while, we finally depart.
We roll down the aisles with a stocked liquor cart.
"Would you like a drink?" "Yes, I'll have three.
A pillow, a blanket, do you have ice tea?"

It's time for the meals and I'm slinging the hash
Then I'll be back to thank you for trash.
Choice of the day is dine or decline,
And if you don't mind, let us serve the "whine."

We finally land and we're happier now.
We got through this flight, just don't know how.
"Buh Bye, Buh Bye and have a nice day,
Sorry about the two-hour delay."

So you may ask, why do I fly?
Doing this job, mile high in the sky?
I could be a plumber or work in a bank
But this life's the best and that's being Frank!

Life's a journey, not a destination, I say,
Try to enjoy the flight, not dread it away.
Whether business, pleasure, or if things should go wrong
Remember that both life and your journey, are not all that
long.

An Airline Product

My mother was a stewardess in the days when it was required that they also be registered nurses. At the time it was truly a glamorous job — gloves, hats, and the birth of the jet engine. My father was an airline ramp agent working his way through law school. Instead of finding her traditional pilot, my mother married the young baggage handler. It was against the rules for stewardesses to be married back then, so she quit and had me instead of traveling the world. A silly rule that I guess I should be thankful for. I was actually conceived on one of my mother's last layovers. My father became a wealthy lawyer and while away on business had an affair with a flight attendant, which brought the end of a 14-year marriage. Two of my next five stepmothers were also flight attendants (the flight attendant attraction must run in the family).

I joined the airline with adventure in my eyes. I found the love of my life on a layover and married her thereafter.

We both continue to work in the airline industry, as do all my friends. My mother uses the free travel passes more than I do. I have written a couple of books about air travel and have paid most of my living expenses with airline wages.

One could say the airlines have been very good to my family and me and, while I mock the absurdities involved, I fully realize this point.

Perhaps my kids will be interested in the same industry as their potential future, but I will do my best to steer them away from this endeavor, even though I will probably fail. I undoubtedly owe a lot of gratitude to my airline, but I would like to think they owe me a little bit of thanks as well.

I love most everything about this profession. I love the interesting people I work with and the intriguing people I serve. I enjoy the anticipation of waking up in a different city or country, and then returning home to my family. Believe it or not, I enjoy the littlest details, from trying to accommodate every passenger's meal choice to assisting with itinerary problems.

I believe in attaining knowledge of the world and if thanking you for your trash furthers this goal, then I willingly oblige. I have said it many times before, but I will say it once again — the true joy in life is the journey. If I have made your journey slightly more joyful, then I have done my job.

It appears my long-term plans of being a flight attendant while doing another job will be cut short by the financial roller coaster in the sky. The airline industry's future is uncertain and a bit gloomy, so I am in the process of looking for a "real job." Oh, the horror of it all.

When anyone asks me at some future time about my former career as a flight attendant I will tell them what a great time I had; in fact I guess I could say that I wrote the book on it. I will try to carry the concept of "being Frank" wherever I go in life. Who knows, maybe I will even write another book on my next job, but somehow A. Frank Programmer doesn't have a distinctive ring to it.

So, if this is the end of the line for me in this profession, I would truly like to say it has been my pleasure serving, observing, and flying with you. Be Frank, enjoy the journey, and as a wise old Indian man once said, "from the heart of my bottom,"

BUH BYE!

The Author

A. Frank Steward has worked as a flight attendant with two major international carriers during the past fifteen years. The author of *The Air Traveler's Survival Guide* (September 2001), Frank holds a bachelor's degree in computer science from a London university and has had a wide variety of jobs spanning continents: jazz trumpet player, bartender, waiter, computer programmer, and writer for a newspaper. He continues to fly and write about "the people I meet at thirty-five thousand feet." For the past ten years he has been happily married to 'Martha', who is also employed by the airlines, starting as a flight attendant and now is a pilot. They live on the East Coast together with their five cats.

Travel Resources

The following books can be ordered directly from the publisher. Complete this form (or list the titles), include your name and address, enclose payment, and send your order to:

IMPACT PUBLICATIONS
9104 Manassas Drive, Suite N
Manassas Park, VA 20111-5211 (USA)
Tel. 1-800-361-1055 (orders only)
703-361-7300 (information) Fax 703-335-9486
E-mail: info@impactpublications.com
Online bookstore: www.impactpublications.com

All prices are in US dollars. Orders from individuals should be prepaid by check, money order, or credit card (Visa, MasterCard, American Express, and Discover). We accept credit card orders by telephone, fax, email, and online. If your order must be shipped outside the United States, please include an additional US $2.00 per title for surface mail or the appropriate air mail rate for books weighing 24 ounces each. Orders usually ship within 48 hours. For more information on the author, travel resources, and international shopping, visit www.impactpublications.com and www.ishoparoundtheworld.com.

Qty.	Titles	Price	TOTAL

Books By A. Frank Steward

____	The Air Traveler s Survival Guide	$14.95	_____
____	The Plane Truth	$14.95	_____

Other Travel-Related Guides With Impact

____	Best Resumes and CVs for International Jobs	$24.95	_____
____	Jobs for Travel Lovers	$19.95	_____
____	Stone Gods, Wooden Elephants	$14.95	_____
____	The Traveling Woman	$14.95	_____
____	Travel Planning on the Internet	$19.95	_____
____	Treasures and Pleasures of Australia	$17.95	_____
____	Treasures and Pleasures of China	$14.95	_____
____	Treasures and Pleasures of Egypt	$16.95	_____
____	Treasures and Pleasures of Hong Kong	$16.95	_____
____	Treasures and Pleasures of India	$16.95	_____
____	Treasures and Pleasures of Mexico	$19.95	_____

___ Treasures and Pleasures of Morocco	$17.95	_____
___ Treasures and Pleasures of New Mexico	$19.95	_____
___ Treasures and Pleasures of Rio/Sao Paulo	$13.95	_____
___ Treasures and Pleasures of Singapore/Bali	$16.95	_____
___ Treasures and Pleasures of Southern Africa	$19.95	_____
___ Treasures and Pleasures of Thailand	$19.95	_____
___ Treasures and Pleasures of Turkey	$16.95	_____
___ Treasures and Pleasures of Vietnam and Cambodia	$16.95	_____

SUBTOTAL ------------ $ _____

■ Virginia residents add 4.5% sales tax $ _____

■ Shipping/handling ($5.00 for the first title and $2.00 for each additional book) $ _____

■ Additional amount if shipping outside U.S. $ _____

TOTAL ENCLOSED ------------- $ _____

SHIP TO:

Name_____

Address_____

_____

_____

Phone Number_____

PAYMENT METHOD:

❑ I enclose check/money order for $ _____

made payable to IMPACT PUBLICATIONS

❑ Please charge $ _____ to my credit card:

❑ Visa ❑ MasterCard ❑ American Express ❑ Discover

Card # _____

Expiration Date: _____/_____

Signature _____

Keep in Touch . . .
On the Web!

www.impactpublications.com
www.ishoparoundtheworld.com
www.hoteltravelshop.com
www.mycruiseshop.com
www.contentfortravel.com
www.winningthejob.com
www.veteransworld.com
www.contentforcareers.com